THE LOSER LIST

REVENGE OF THE LOSER

Written and Illustrated by

H.N. KOWITT

SCHOLASTIC PRESS / NEW YORK

ISBN 978-0-545-42611-4

Text copyright © 2012 by Holly Kowitt
Illustrations copyright © 2012 by Scholastic Inc.
All rights reserved. Published by Scholastic Press,
an imprint of Scholastic Inc., Publishers since 1920.
SCHOLASTIC, SCHOLASTIC PRESS, and associated logos are
trademarks and/or registered trademarks of Scholastic Inc.

12 11 10 9 8 7 6 5 4 3 2 1   12 13 14 15 16 17/0

Printed in the U.S.A.   40
This edition first printing, January 2012

To the one, the only,
David Manis

Special thanks to
Ellen Miles

* ME AT-A-GLANCE

Name: Danny Shine (rhymes with "whine")
Age: 12
School: Gerald Ford Middle School
Likes: M&M pancakes, Asia O'Neill
Dislikes: Gym class, chili squares
Obsession: Comics
Secret fear: Being picked last in volleyball
Most embarrassing moment: Getting caught in the girls' bathroom
Favorite compliment: "I like the way you draw vomit."

* CHAPTER ONE *

Ty Randall must die.

That's what I vowed as I sat in the cafeteria, watching him take over the lunch table, the school, and the only girl I ever liked. After an excruciating hour, I'd had about all I could take.

And I'd started lunch period feeling good. Really good. I had just finished drawing my new comic book, and couldn't wait to show it to Emma, Morgan, Sophie, and Kendra. As I looked around for Jasper, I patted my backpack to make sure it was still there.

Drawing is what I live for, pretty much. There's nothing like getting the stink lines on a smelly sock just right, and hearing the girl next to me in pre-alg say, "Wow — did you copy that out of a book, or something?"

"Yo, Danny!" My best friend, Jasper, shouted across the cafeteria. We'd eaten lunch together almost every day since we started Gerald Ford Middle School. I like how he does his own thing, no matter how unpopular it is — having a toy band, chess-boxing, or collecting weird animals.

* JASPER AT-A-GLANCE

Personality: Freakishly
    smart
Goal: To put a vending
    machine in his
    locker
Wears: Two different-colored
    sneakers
Eats: Swedish Fish ("for the
    riboflavin")
**Ratio of action figures to
    friends:** 8 to 1

    For the fifth day in a row, he'd nailed us a spot at a table I thought of as Semi-Normal, a step up from our usual spot at Tech Geeks. It was mostly girls, and they didn't seem to be an official clique. They're not the ones writing hottie lists in the second floor bathroom. They're the ones you'd want as your lab partner, or sitting behind you in percussion ensemble.

Sophie De Mano

Reputation: Likeable gum-chewer

Enjoys: Wacky Wednesdays

Emma Priestly

Reputation: Bookish, semi-funny

Last read: More Dog Stories

Morgan Chatterjee

Reputation: Mad scrapbooker

AKA: "Picasso with unicorn stickers"

Kendra Maxtone-Cousins

Reputation: Cute overachiever

Screensaver: Insects of the world

I kept waiting for someone to stop Jasper and me from sitting there. On the food chain at school, we're a quarter of the way up. We're not outcasts, but no one's texting us about the latest party, either.

* FIVE TEXTS I'VE NEVER GOTTEN:

going 2 Jenna's? Shld b ragin

Awesome touchdown! U ROCK!!!!!!!!!

Nice 'stache.

so danny give it up Boxrs or briefs?

U r brutally hot

The girls at the table seemed to tolerate us, even if they didn't exactly talk to us. The moment we slap our trays down, I'm always nervous. Would we get away with it again? As I hovered near the table, Emma looked up from her book. She moved over to make room, and my chest felt lighter. We were in.

"So, Petrokis and I were debating best superpower. . . ."

This was Jasper's idea of a good opener. He doesn't get that you have to talk differently when girls are around. They don't want to hear about the latest sci-fi movie, and in what direction it reeked.

"He said mind control." Jasper bit into a sandwich. "But I said —"

That sent Emma straight back to her book.

Meanwhile, I was plotting out my big Vampire Slugs reveal. I couldn't

just say, "Look what I did!". No, it had to be more offhand. . . .

    I reach for a sandwich, and Vampire Slugs spills out of my backpack. Emma picks it up, intrigued. "What's this?"

    "Oh, 's nothing," I say, but Emma swipes it and reads every word.

    "You . . . you drew this?"

    I shrug modestly. Now Morgan and Sophie are straining for a look. . . .

    "Danny!" Jasper thumped me on the arm. "Did you even hear what I said?"

    "I missed the part about teleporting."

    As he launched into his rant, I slapped my backpack on the table. Time to unveil my masterpiece. I tilted the backpack to release the comic. Nothing came out — just crumbs. Where was it? I turned the backpack upside down, and THWAP! A torrent of paper, garbage, and Cool Ranch Doritos blasted the table.

    Emma gasped. "You're getting chips all over me!"

    "GEEZ." Morgan sighed.

Even Jasper asked, "What are you doing?"

"Trying to find my . . . um . . ." I tried to think of something cool. "Frisbee."

"Frisbee?" Jasper repeated.

Where was the freakin' comic? I stuck my hand in — Vampire Slugs was wedged in a side pocket. I pulled it out violently, spraying more Doritos, and kicking off another round of cries.

"Danny!" Morgan brushed off her shirt, and Sophie sighed.

Now everyone was mad. But . . . there it was.

"Is that your new comic?" Jasper reached for it.

"What comic?" Despite her annoyance, Emma sounded curious.

Jasper held <u>Vampire Slugs</u> up so everyone could see it.

Just like I'd hoped!

"Is this the sequel to <u>Mutant Maggots With Bad Breath</u>?" asked Jasper.

"No!" I said. The title was embarrassing. "That was, like, a million years ago."

"Hey." Sophie pointed to an X-ray monster. "This is kind of funny."

YESSS!!

This was <u>it</u> — the moment I'd been waiting for. "See, my major influences are —" I leaned in.

Emma's and Sophie's heads turned. "TY!!!" they called out.

A tall guy with caramel-colored hair and rimless glasses sailed by. He stopped and blinked, as if trying to remember who they were.

"Okay if I sit here?" He was out of breath. "No room at the other table." He pointed to a bunch of soccer players.

The girls fell over each other to clear a spot.

"Definitely!" "Right here!" "Plenty o' space!"

Emma's leg pushed against me. "Move over."

"Who's Ty?" Jasper chomped a French fry.

"Ty Randall." Emma lowered her voice. "The new guy. From California."

I'd seen him around, talking earnestly. My coolness radar — "cool-dar" — pegged him as someone to watch out for. New kids in school usually have to prove themselves — by getting into a fight, mouthing off to a teacher, or hitting a long home run. But he seemed pre-approved, somehow.

As soon as he sat down, the energy changed abruptly. The girls started fidgeting with their headbands, bracelets, or juice boxes. Everyone's eyes were glued to Ty.

It was maddening.

He dumped his stuff on the table: a slim notebook — not the clunky spiral kind our moms

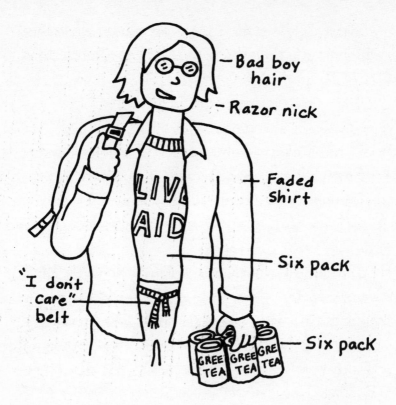

Bad boy hair

Razor nick

Faded Shirt

LIV AID

Six pack

"I don't care" belt

GREE TEA GREE TEA GRE TEA

Six pack

bought us, but a leather bound one with graph paper. A brightly colored CD tumbled out, and some leafy thing wrapped in tinfoil.

"Eggplant burrito," he explained, while people stared.

My stomach sank. How could I get everyone's attention back?

"Hey, Ty." Morgan pointed to Ty's CD. "What's that?"

"Sierra Leone All Stars," he said. "Awesome."

Sophie tilted her head. "I think I've heard of them."

Right.

"Yeah?" Ty bit into his burrito. "You like world music?"

There were excited murmurs. "For sure," Morgan said loudly. Suddenly they were all great fans.

* WHAT'S (PROBABLY) IN TY'S BACKPACK

Healthy   Natural fibers   Non-violent
snacks   tube sock   video games

Ty sighed. "I hope there'll be African drumming in Green-a-palooza," he said. Everyone leaned in to hear more. "It's this Earth Day festival I'm putting on with different acts about the environment and global warming."

More oohs and ahhhs. Was there anything this guy wouldn't do to impress girls?

"That's so great," Emma breathed, nodding her head strenuously.

"Student council could help," said Kendra.

I broke into a sweat. How could we get off climate change and back to <u>Vampire Slugs</u>? Ty had hijacked my one moment of glory! Those girls had been complimenting my stuff before he showed up. Picking up the comic, I waited for an opening.

"Where will it be held, Ty?"

"You need volunteers?"

I had to jump in.

"So, Vampire Slugs, yeah, it was just this idea I had. . . ." I must have been shouting, because everyone turned.

"Hey," Ty pointed at me. "Let me see that."

A second later, I realized Ty meant my comic book. I passed it to him, hoping that would get the girls' attention. Their eyes grazed the cover as it traveled down the table.

Ty didn't crack a smile as he paged through it. "I never saw a plant with teeth before."

"Guess you don't get around much." I shrugged.

"So, about this festival . . ." Emma said.

"Yeah! Sorry." He tossed the book back to me, ending the world debut of Vampire Slugs. I left it on the table, in case anyone else wanted to see it. Hopeful, I looked around: Emma? Sophie?

My chest felt very heavy, all of a sudden.

Ty blabbed on about Stupid-palooza. Never before had such kickin' entertainment been lined up for such a worthy cause. It would single-handedly reverse the melting of the Arctic ice cap, end world hunger, and cure cancer. Or something like that.

All I knew was I'd drawn the greatest comic of my life, and no one was looking at it.

"Green-a-pa-WHAT?" Chantal came up to the table, catching the tail end of Ty's rant. She's the biggest diva in our class, a major

 busybody, and the self-appointed boss of seventh grade. If some big event was going on, she had to be in on it. "What's this I hear about a show?"

"It's an Earth Day Festival," Ty said.

"You need singers for that?" She raised an eyebrow.

"Sure," Ty said. "The music'll be traditional. You know — folk songs."

Chantal stroked her chin. "You call Beyoncé traditional?"

"Um —" He coughed.

"Yo, Ty —"

"TY!"

People kept coming up to him. How had he gotten so well-known already? More people had talked to Ty during lunch than had talked to me since the start of middle school. I felt completely invisible.

"Hey . . . Ty?"

I knew that voice.

Whoa.

<u>Double whoa.</u>

It was Asia O'Neill, my secret crush. She was looking good in one of her weird outfits — a baseball jacket and ballet slippers. I don't know her well, but she's always carrying around something interesting.

She's smart, impatient, and a little sarcastic.

When I saw her tap Ty on the shoulder, I looked away. Direct eye contact was out of the question.

"About the Green-a-palooza article," Asia said to Ty. "I wanted to follow up."

"Yeah," Ty said, smiling up at her.

"Could we do the interview in Free Period?"

"I — definitely." Ty was still smiling.

WHAT??

My mind raced to take it all in. He knew Asia? It was one thing watching the girls at the table drool all over him, but ... Asia?

This took it to a whole new level.

Ty was facing her now, saying something about "building awareness." And now she was nodding and smiling. Did this guy know how pompous he sounded? I couldn't believe Asia was swallowing it.

"Yeah, Ty," she said. "That's so true."

I couldn't take it! I kicked Jasper under the table.

"Ow!" he said. "What was that for?"

I felt my face get hot. My crush on Asia is so unmentionable, I've never even told <u>him</u>. So of course, he didn't get it.

It wasn't fair. I'd liked Asia since the first day of middle school, when I saw her in a striped shirt, quietly reading a graphic novel.

She seemed quirky, interesting, and mysterious, someone who wouldn't be interested in the typical kind of guy. If a girl was ever going to like me, it would be someone like her.

So why did the one girl I could maybe hit it off with have to fall under Ty's spell too?

My heart was beating like crazy.

"Hey — I've got this comic I just drew," I blurted out in desperation. Asia and Ty seemed startled.

I looked on the table, but it was gone. Frantically, I started moving sandwiches and napkins around. Where was it? Finally, I spotted a slice of the familiar yellow cover on the floor. YES! Reaching down to grab it, I realized that it was stuck — wadded under someone's hiking boot.

Emma was standing on it.

I yelped and she moved her foot, apologizing.

My fantastic comic was completely trashed!

I felt like sobbing as I picked up the mangled papers.

Oh, man.

That's when I vowed to come up with my own brilliant project — something so big, so global, and so important, no one at school could ignore it. An event that would make Asia interview <u>me</u> for <u>Happenings</u>, the hard-hitting, take-no-prisoners newspaper of Gerald Ford Middle School.

Something that would make Asia look into my eyes and say, "Yeah, Danny. That's soooo true."

* CHAPTER TWO *

On my way home from school with Jasper, I brought up the subject of doing our own megaproject. We could raise money for an excellent cause — like sending the whole class on a great field trip.

"Since when do you organize school events?" asked Jasper, as we trudged down the street. "You hate stuff like Spring Fling."

Well — yeah. "I'm talking about something cooler," I insisted. Actually, I didn't know what I was talking about. I just knew it had to get people talking about something other than Green-a-palooza. "I just thought — why don't we have a class trip to someplace decent for once, instead of History Village?"

Greetings from
HISTORY VILLAGE
" WHERE FUN GOES TO DIE "

"Hnnnh." Jasper nodded.

"Wouldn't you like to go someplace cool?" I asked. "Somewhere you actually <u>wanted</u> to go?"

I tried to imagine some dream field trips.

Museum of
Video Games

Crocodile
Wrestling Match

Monster Trucks on Ice Show

We passed a playground with a tube slide, and watched a toddler come shooting out. "Hey!" I suddenly had an idea. "Big Kahuna Water Park."

"YESSS!" Jasper pumped his fist. "I always wanted to ride Death Wish."

"How 'bout the Twisted Tunnel of Terror?"

We both started mimicking the radio ads, talking a mile-a-minute like the crazed announcer:

"GO GO GO to Big Kahuna Water Park for some butt-kicking, pulse-poundin', jaw droppin', blood-curdlin' splashtastic fun. Are you crazy enough to try the Devil's Squirt Gun? How 'bout rides like Big Barracuda or Monsoon Madness? Don't come unless you're INSAAAAAAAAAAAAANE!!!!!!!!!!!!"

When we spat out the last words, we burst out laughing. I could almost feel the spray of cold water on my face as we bolted down the Honolulu Hurricane, a four-story mammoth wave before "free-falling" to the splash pool below. What a perfect thing to do when the weather got better. . . .

I could see Jasper had caught the fever too. His eyes looked glazed, and I could see him mentally barreling through a six-story waterslide. We were both sweating.

"Well? Wouldn't that be cool?" I nudged him.

"Uhhh-hunh." Jasper wiped his brow. "But tix are 25 dollars. For a hundred and thirty seventh graders, it'd cost . . . 3,250 dollars. Plus transportation." He was super quick at math. "That's a lot of Rice Krispie squares. Why don't we just make our parents take us?"

"No." My voice rose. "They'll never get around to it. If we organize a class trip, it's a sure thing. Plus —" I took a breath. "We'll get props from everyone. Look how they slobbered over Ty today." My voice broke when I said his name.

"I don't know," Jasper said with a frown. "How would we raise all that money, really?"

"We'll think of something." I waved my hand. "Ice cream social. Guitar Hero contest. Car wash."

"Too much work." Jasper scowled.

"Yeah, but —" I was pulling out every stop. "Think of that sixty-foot vertical drop in <u>total darkness</u>."

He gulped. "Uhhnnh —"

I smiled, and slapped him on the back. "Knew you'd come around."

At lunch the next day, Ty was back. After seeing how in demand he was, I figured he'd find a better spot to dump his solar-paneled backpack. The girls at our table weren't super-popular types, but Ty didn't seem to care where he sat. I guess if you're cool enough, it doesn't matter.

When Jasper and I sat down, we caught the end of Ty's story.

"... helping out at the marine habitat, really getting close to the sea life..."

That was fun to picture.

Everyone was so caught up in his story, even Jasper didn't notice when I rolled my eyes. God, that guy could go on. But this time, I wasn't going to let Ty take over; I had my own little bomb to drop.

"Hey, Jasper," I said. "What rides are you going to do at Big Kahuna?"

Sophie's eyes strayed over to us.

"I dunno," he said. "Maybe the Mega-Twister."

I rubbed my chin. "I was thinking Honolulu Hurricane."

Emma turned halfway around. "Who's going to Big Kahuna?" she asked.

"We all are." I tried to sound casual. "The whole seventh grade. Jasper and I are organizing a field trip."

Ty stopped talking, and everyone looked at us.

"Do you have permission?" Kendra asked, sitting down. She was kind of a goody-goody.

"Not yet," I admitted. "We have to raise the money first." This was the haziest part of the plan. "We're batting around a few ideas."

"We'd get the whole class on board," I continued. "You know, raising money for it."

"Interesting." Ty nodded. "If you need help fund-raising, I did a lot of that at my old school."

"Thanks, but — we're set. Except for the money part," I added. Jasper kicked me under the table.

"Oh." Ty looked confused.

"My older brother went to Big Kahuna last summer," said Sophie. "They had to stop a ride 'cuz he barfed in the raft."

"Awesome," said Jasper.

"Hey, Donny," Ty started again.

"Danny."

"Sorry. About your, uh, idea — Can I make a suggestion?"

I shook my head, but Jasper said, "Sure."

"Big Kahuna sounds neat," he said. "I miss the ocean, and I'm up for any wave, even fake ones. But . . ." He paused. "Would you think about — doing a fund-raiser that has, um, more of an upside?"

"Up . . . side?" I stammered.

"There are so many things to do." Ty's words tumbled out. "How about renovating a playground in a poor neighborhood? My aunt teaches at P.S. 160 in the city. Their equipment is really run down, and if you could raise five thousand dollars, they'd be able to fix up the whole place."

Jasper and I looked at each other. Outside, I tried to look calm, but inside I was cursing Ty.

"Gosh, Ty, that'd be so cool," Kendra said. Emma and Sophie nodded admiringly, and I swear Morgan batted her eyelashes at him.

Ty smiled sheepishly. "Just a thought."

"Awesome," Sophie added.

"Seriously." Morgan sighed.

But...!

But...!

But...!

The whole point was to go to the freakin' water park! To give us something to look forward to, after a year of pie charts and decimals and Salute to Semicolons worksheets. A place where we could forget everything for a few hours, eat caramel corn, and get soaking wet.

Was that too much to ask?

After Ty's little speech, saying no wasn't even an <u>option</u>. Only the most petty, selfish, low-down person would choose the wrong one:

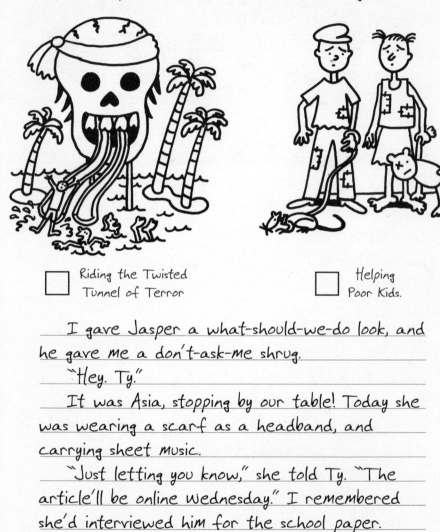

☐ Riding the Twisted
Tunnel of Terror

☐ Helping
Poor Kids.

I gave Jasper a what-should-we-do look, and he gave me a don't-ask-me shrug.

"Hey. Ty."

It was Asia, stopping by our table! Today she was wearing a scarf as a headband, and carrying sheet music.

"Just letting you know," she told Ty. "The article'll be online Wednesday." I remembered she'd interviewed him for the school paper.

"Thanks," he said.

"Now, Danny..." Emma had turned to me. "About this playground..."

Asia's ears seemed to prick up. "What playground?"

"A playground for poor kids," Sophie told her. "Danny and Jasper are raising money to renovate one."

"Really?" Asia looked over, blinking like she'd never noticed me before. "You're doing that?" I tried to concentrate on the question, and not the citrus-y smell of her hair.

"Uh, yeah." I stood up straighter. "We might ... do that."

"Renovate a playground?" Jasper gulped. "Gee, guys, I don't —"

Ty, Asia, and the girls at the table stared at him.

"... rule it out," he mumbled.

"Wow." Asia nodded approvingly. "That's amazing."

Oh, man.

Ty stood up and shot me a look. "When you decide on a fund-raiser, let me know." He stuffed his garbage into a paper bag. "I've got an F4F meeting."

"What's that?" Sophie asked in a singsong voice.

"Food 4 Folks." Ty pulled on his backpack. "We use skateboards to bring meals to homebound seniors." He held up his hand. "Ciao."

Asia took off, and the girls at the table watched Ty roll through the lunchroom, until the glass doors swung behind him.

Jasper and I looked at each other.

What just happened? Somehow I'd just gotten guilted into throwing a fund-raiser for Ty's cause. Why didn't I say, "No! I'm sticking to my idea — a class trip to the water park"? What an idiot I was! Now I'd never get to ride the Honolulu Hurricane.

And — more important —

How on earth were we going to raise 5,000 dollars?

* CHAPTER THREE *

I had no idea how to raise money. Since middle school I'd successfully avoided being involved in any kind of Plant Sale or Bowl-a-Thon. I cursed Ty for getting us into this mess, but I knew it was my own fault for wanting to impress Asia. Walking home from school, Jasper laid into me.

"What now?" His face was all red. "The whole point was to go to the water park. And even _that_ I wasn't sure about! At least, not the fund-raising part." He fumed some more. "This is way, WAY out of our league. This is crazy!"

I felt my stomach rumble. "Maybe if we don't mention the playground, people will forget about it."

"Well, I don't care what they say. I'm

not doing it." Jasper was indifferent to public embarrassment, which I respected.

Usually.

I had other things to think about — like the upcoming art contest. Every year, Gerald Ford holds a school art contest called "Expressions". The title's lame, but there's a prize — 500 dollars — and winning entries from each class get displayed at Fudge for Less.

The next day, before classes started, I checked out the competition. The entries were lined up in the Media Room until the winners were announced on Friday. Two days isn't long to wait, but it felt like forever.

I scanned the room quickly, skipping past the sculpture to the paintings:

"Still Life with Dishwashing Liquid"

"Giant Wad of Money"

"SpongeBob"

And then, finally, mine:

"I Was a Preteen Cyclops"

My cartoon stood out, but I knew that winning the contest wasn't a slam dunk. The judges could easily pick "Still Life with Dishwashing Liquid" or Randy Castro's "Mixed Media Porsche X-380". I saw Brady Spitzer stopped in front of mine, and he held his palm up for a high five.

"Dude." He slapped my hand. "This is deeply, deeply twisted."

I nodded, pleased. A pair of girls wandered into the room, and a girl in a polo shirt pointed to my drawing and said, "Awesome."

Wow — a compliment from someone who didn't even know me!

I looked at Randy Castro's Porsche again. He was the only guy in seventh grade who was a better artist than me, and I had to admire how realistic the car looked. But his painting was clearly taken from an ad photo; mine was more creative.

"Hey, Danny," Emma said, coming up behind me. "Cool drawing."

"Thanks." I blushed.

This day was getting better and better!

I walked to class with a burst of energy, thinking about those compliments. I was the class

artist. People thought my stuff was great. I'd probably win the art contest.

So why did I let Ty get to me? We were just good at different things. He rocked at do-gooder activities, making sappy speeches, and impressing girls. I was good at drawing. I could live with that.

There was nothing to be jealous of.

That day at lunch, I kept it together while Ty was talking about animal rescue activities. I even asked him a question — after being Art Star that morning, I could afford to be generous. The next day, he sat at the soccer table, so it wasn't even an issue. Maybe the Ty Problem was taking care of itself.

On Friday I woke up early, excited to hear the art contest results at our weekly assembly. Knowing I might be called up to the podium, I wore my best clothes.

Best T-shirt   Best socks   Lucky underwear

What would I say in my acceptance speech? On the Grammy awards, winners were always thanking Jesus, and other artists who inspired them. I could talk about Krazy Karl, creator of Rat Girl.

And of course, I couldn't help thinking about the prize money.

* FIVE DUMBEST WAYS TO SPEND $500

1. Solid gold backpack
2. Return 250 library books a week late
3. 2,000 quarters for video arcade
4. Bet whole thing on 7th/8th grade football game
5. Twizzlers

But what if I didn't win? There was a very good chance, an <u>excellent</u> chance, that Randy Castro's sports car would be decorating the restaurant, not my Cyclops.

When I met Jasper at the bus stop, he asked, "What'll you do with the money?"

"It's not a done deal," I said. "Randy Castro could —"

"His stuff isn't nearly as deranged as yours."

Jasper rocked.

When I got to school, a few people wished me luck. Some just assumed I was going to win. Somehow I stumbled through the day, spacing out in English class, taking the wrong staircase to gym, and dropping papers all over the floor during Math. The art contest was all I could think about.

    I couldn't wait until 11:45, when the assembly started.

    Sitting down next to Jasper, I tapped my pen against the armrest.

    "Settle down, people," Dr. Kulbarsh, the principal, boomed from the stage. He cleared his throat and gave us his we-can-take-all-day-if-we-need-to smile.

    "First item on the agenda," he began. "Positive Behavior During Pep Rallies."

    Everyone groaned, and I slyly took out my pen, like I was taking notes. Of course, I was really just doodling.

   After listening to Kulbarsh drone on endlessly,
I finally heard words that made my head
snap up.
   "Now, the part you've all been waiting for."
He paused. "There were over a hundred
entries, each wonderful in their own way.
Whoever participated, give yourself a hand."
   I tapped my pen halfheartedly on the
armrest.
   "And the winner is . . ." Kulbarsh looked at
his index card and chuckled.
   I shifted forward, bouncing on my toes.
Jasper nudged me.
   "Ty Randall!"

* CHAPTER FOUR *

WHAT?????

I couldn't believe my ears. Ty flew down the aisle, and I realized I was halfway to standing up. I sank back in my seat, mortified.

The principal held an oblong piece of junk with wheels on it. Ty shook his hand breezily, like he received awards on a daily basis.

"Ty," said the principal. "Tell us about this."

"Sure." Ty's voice got deeper. "It's a scooter made out of recycled materials: cardboard, newspaper, water bottles, crushed cans."

"Isn't that something." Kulbarsh nodded. "The jury was impressed by the message about reducing waste."

Thunderous applause. "But this is an _art_ contest!" I whispered to Jasper. "Not an environmental competition!"

I felt like my chest had dropped to the floor. I knew I might not win the contest, but I never thought I'd lose it to —

Ty.

I tried to paste a smile on my face, and clap with everyone else. When the assembly ended, I moved out of the auditorium like a robot. Just my luck, Chantal was one of the first people to talk to me.

"Danny, are you gonna let that soccer-playin' string bean take away your prize?" She shook her head. "If I were you, I'd beat him up."

"Ha-ha." I chuckled awkwardly, aware people were listening.

Who even knew he _did_ artwork? I thought he was busy saving the world! And since when is a heap of garbage glued together considered art? I hadn't seen his entry, since I'd skipped past the craft projects in the Multi-Purpose Room. Usually they weren't known for bold artistic statements:

Walking down the hall, Jasper gave me a sympathy punch. "You got shafted," he said. "Those morons don't appreciate comic art genius."

I nodded, waiting for more outrage. We walked for a few moments in silence. Finally, Jasper spoke again. "I wonder what he used to attach the wheels."

Even Jasper couldn't help admiring Ty.

I almost blew off lunch that day, not wanting to hear any more about Ty's brilliant project. But when I looked around the lunchroom, Ty was sitting with his soccer buddies. Good. I could sit at our usual spot without having to face him.

I'd still have to face everyone else.

When my lunch tray hit the table, Emma looked up. "Hey, Danny. Sorry about —" She swallowed. "You know." I saw her and Morgan exchange glances. "The art contest."

I managed a shrug. "'S okay."

"Yours was good." Emma nodded.

"Thanks," I mumbled.

No one said anything for a few moments.

Then Sophie sat down and looked around. "Did someone die, or something?"

Eventually, conversation started up again. Morgan talked about a scrapbooking slumber party she wanted to have, and Jasper and I debated Best Movie Explosions.

"Hey," Ty said, joining our table. Conversation came to a halt.

My chest tightened up, watching him accept high fives. The important thing was to act normal. Jasper and I exchanged looks, and Ty nodded at us stiffly.

"I can't believe you made a scooter," Morgan gushed.

"What'll you do with the money?" Sophie asked, letting her smile linger.

"Donate it." Ty shrugged. "Greenpeace, maybe, or —"

I got up abruptly, not wanting to hear any more. Of course he'd give it away unselfishly, and let everyone know. I had planned to spend my prize money at the Apple Store. Once again, Ty had made me feel small.

My head was about to explode. Not knowing what to do, I headed for the vending machine and stood there.

"I recommend Reese's Pieces." Jasper was standing next to me.

My mouth tightened. I took a deep breath.

"Ty's got to be stopped," I said grimly. "Before he takes over the whole freakin' school."

Jasper stepped away from me and blinked. "Well, I wouldn't say —"

"Green-a-palooza? The art prize?!" I was practically spitting. "He hasn't even been at Ford two months! He's become, like," I searched for the right word, "a — disease, or something. He's got to be taken down!"

"Whoa." Jasper pushed back his glasses. "Aren't you getting a little carried away? I mean, you should have won the art prize... but —" He shrugged. "He's not this evil force, or anything. He's okay."

"OKAY????" I was boiling. "He's INSUFFERABLE!"

Jasper frowned. "Really? I thought he was kind of a nice guy."

ARRRRRRRRRRRRRGGGHHHHHH!!!!

My face was burning up, and people were looking at us. I stormed out of the lunchroom and shoved my face into the nearest drinking fountain.

I found Ty infuriating. But apparently, that was something I'd have to keep to myself.

* CHAPTER FIVE *

Ty's name didn't come up for a few days.

Jasper and I avoided the subject. Instead, we stuck to our usual topics: comic books, movies, video games. We were at his house after school, working on my new e-comic. Jasper was helping me put it online so I could post weekly installments.

"Congratulations," said Jasper, pushing a button. We were at his house, after school. "The site's live."

"Excellent," I said.

"Let's take a break," he said, stretching out. He started flipping channels. A Spanish soap opera, a car commercial, a Western in black-and-white, a news report . . .

"Hey." I pointed. "That's our school!"

What was it doing on TV? Jasper turned up the volume. "... new science lab at Gerald Ford Middle School. We're talking to student Ty Randall about the facility."

"TY?!" we both yelled.

"...state-of-the-art," Ty said. "More sinks, more room. You don't have to wait to use a microscope."

"Of all people to interview..." Jasper frowned. "Why him?"

"What are you working on?" asked the newscaster.

"A solar oven."

Ty held up something cardboard. "Made out of a pizza box."

"Wow!" The newscaster's hair looked like a stiff, blond helmet. "What have you baked?"

"Chocolate chip cookies," Ty said, looking sheepish. "My mom helped."

"Are you entering the science fair?" the newswoman demanded. "Sounds like you're the guy to beat!"

"Dunno," Ty mumbled. "Haven't thought about it."

Oh, <u>sure</u> you haven't.

The camera shot back to an anchorman at a desk, who whistled. "This kid is really going places. And he's only in seventh grade! With their new facility, Gerald Ford Middle School is sure to turn out more stars like him."

"Ron — what were you inventing at that age?" asked a co-anchor.

"Excuses to avoid homework!" he joked. "Let's check weekend weather...."

"Why didn't they interview _me_? Why wasn't I there?" Jasper shook his head. "I could have shown Robot Dog."

Jasper was the school's best science student, hands-down. Teachers called him when they had computer trouble. He'd won the science fair last year, and would probably win it again with one of his wacky projects.

Robot Dog was Jasper's latest invention, a mechanical hound that ate toy trucks and cars. Sometimes it got confused and chomped a stapler. I liked how Robot Dog's eyes lit up when he sank his teeth into a Hot Wheels Humvee Power Set.

"I dunno." Now it was my turn to be calm. "Maybe they just showed up and he was there."

"Ha!" Jasper snarled. "I bet he set it up."

He was finally getting it! Now I wouldn't be the only one with a Ty Problem. Feeling slightly guilty about how well this was working out, I chose my words carefully. "Could be. Who knows?"

"Solar oven," Jasper snorted. "Like _that_ would be hard to make."

I rolled my eyes in solidarity, but actually, I was impressed. Only a genius like Jasper would scoff at a pizza box that baked cookies. But I could see he was feeling the same personal insult that I'd felt when they made that announcement at assembly. It burned, watching someone get what should have been yours.

"Maybe no one saw it," I said halfheartedly.

The next day at school, the clip was shown in every homeroom. My teacher, Mrs. Forrest, played it twice. "I hope you're all very, very proud," she said. "Ty Randall was a wonderful

spokesperson for this school. You should all feel inspired by him."

I nearly barfed.

"How'd he get to be on TV?" demanded Chantal. "My milk carton bird feeder's better than his stupid oven." Even Chantal felt ripped off.

"He just happened to be in the science lab when Channel 8 came," said Mrs. Forrest. "It could have been anyone."

Yeah, but —

Somehow, it was always Ty.

It didn't help that the girls were buzzing about it at lunch. Jasper and I were talking more at the table now, not just "Is that your fork?", but actually joining in the conversation.

"Baking cookies in a pizza box!" Morgan whooped. "Get. Out."

Jasper clenched his teeth. "It's not that hard."

"So cool!" Sophie wailed. "And I missed it!"

This time, Jasper was the one who cringed at all the Ty-worship. It was one thing to hear them gush about his looks or soccer moves. But his science chops?

That was just unfair.

After lunch, we strolled past the main office, passing the display case. Usually it had some boring diorama on Ancient Rome or "Our Friend Wheat."

This time, there was a pizza box.

"Oh, no." Jasper grunted, as we got closer. "Just say it isn't —"

But it was. Along with the pizza box-solar oven, there was a photo of Ty and an index card explaining how it worked. In the photo, he looked like a guy on the cover of a teen mag under the headline, "Ty — You _Know_ You Want Him!"

A low growl came from Jasper.

"It's clobberin' time." He was quoting the Thing.

I felt a surge of hope. It meant Jasper was finally on board. "So you think — ?" I started to ask, just to be sure.

"He's got to be stopped." Jasper's voice was tight.

Yes! I was so ready for this.

"First, we need some intel," I said, my heart already pounding. "Find something he isn't good at."

"On it."

We sealed the deal with our secret handshake, fusing our pinkie fingers behind our backs with extra fury.

Ty Randall was going down.

* CHAPTER SIX *

"Oh, man," Jasper announced the next Friday. "I got _nothin'._"

We were at our "office", a janitor's supply closet we treated like a private conference room. I tried to get comfortable on a giant canister of barf powder; Jasper was slumped on a bucket. Ralph the janitor could show up at any moment, so we had to talk fast.

"What do you mean, 'nothing'?" I couldn't believe it. Jasper had been working on Ty's background check for a solid week. I thought he'd be on this like a bloodhound, tracking down every clue and refusing to give up until he got answers.

"I called my contacts on the West Coast." Jasper sighed. "I read online copies of his old school newspaper. I researched animal rights groups. Want to know what I found?"

His tone was freaking me out.

"Hit me." I braced myself.

He took a deep breath. "It's worse than we thought. At his old school, he started a model UN, a teen crisis hotline, and the Friends of the Planet Club. He organized a mini Live Aid, and a skateboard recycling drive. When he wasn't winning the soccer cup, or running the San Francisco Marathon."

My chest tightened. "Go on."

"He had a 4.7 grade point average, won the Earth Science Medal, the Golden Frisbee, and topped the Best Speller List. He got eighth graders to donate a drinking fountain to a school in Latin America."

"How 'bout — friends and stuff?" I asked, afraid to hear the answer.

"Captain of sixth-grade soccer. Had a house near the ocean that was great for parties."

   "Geez." I felt nauseated. For a minute, I thought: Maybe he really is a superstar, one-in-a-million kid, and we all have to live with that. It was like he was some kind of national treasure, for God's sake.

   When I remembered him sailing up the aisle at assembly, I felt my stomach rumble. "Did he ever mess up?"

   "Sure." Jasper smiled darkly. "His Cultural

Diversity Fair was underattended. And Recycle-a-Tricycle didn't really go anywhere."

"C'mon." I was annoyed. "He must've done something."

"Once he organized a rally to protest school budget cuts." Jasper said. "But it was nonviolent."

"Jasper," I said, trying not to sound irritated. "After all that work — that's ALL you came up with?"

I heard the clang of keys, and knew we had only seconds left.

"He reeks at archery," Jasper said as Ralph burst in.

Thinking about Ty made my brain hurt, so I put him out of my mind. At computer graphics club, Phil Petrokis and I were working on an

animation project about cyborg cheerleaders who destroy the captain of the football team.

After working for an hour trying

to get the pom-poms right, I left the Tech
Center to hit the bathroom.

   The door wouldn't budge. Forgetting they
locked those bathrooms after school, I walked
down the hall to the gym locker room.

   Luckily, the place was empty — just rows of
lockers and a forlorn tube sock. Good — I wasn't
in the mood for jocks whipping towels at each
other. I did a routine check for new graffiti.

555-6230 BARF CRUD
@ Kyle is a Diptard &%#!*
Eat my *#* AXL
* Butt Breath RULES
Smell it
Shannon Stuffs SPAZ MORON

   A noise by the shower stalls told me I wasn't
alone. I bolted for the exit, but a strange sound
stopped me in my tracks. Somebody was talking —
no, someone was singing. I tiptoed closer, trying

to make out the words. Was it some kind of weird . . . rap song?

   "'Cuz I'm mean
   I'm green
   I'm an eco-freak
   I'm Super Teen . . ."

   Why did that voice sound familiar? I stuck my head around the corner to look. His back was to me, but I could see a body jerking back and forth in wild spasms. It took a second to realize he was <u>dancing</u>.
   And another second to realize it was Ty.
   Holy crud.
   With a towel tied around his waist, he was rapping to the mirror. His front teeth jutted over his lower lip, and his eyes had narrowed into slits. Using a water bottle for a mike, he was concentrating fiercely. My mouth dropped open.

   "Global warming u gotta prevent it
   Let's all write postcards to the Senate. . ."

This was the worst rap I'd ever heard! Being tone-deaf was bad enough. But now he was kicking and twitching with his thumbs turned out. I was staring so hard, I didn't realize my backpack had slid down my arm. As I watched Ty strut, it dropped to the ground with a THUD!

"Hey!" Ty yelled. "Who's there?"

I jumped back, startled. Ty flew around the

corner before I could bolt. When he saw me, his eyes almost popped out.

"For God's sake!" His cheeks reddened as he adjusted his towel. "What're you doing here?"

"I was just —" My voice died.

"I didn't know anyone was around," Ty said with a scowl.

"I just got here," I said.

Neither of us spoke for a few seconds. Ty kicked a gym locker, and I picked up my backpack.

"Did you, uh, write that yourself?" I dared to ask.

"Yeah."

More silence.

"Rapping is just, like . . ." Ty looked away. "Kind of a goof." He seemed a little embarrassed, but frankly, not embarrassed enough.

"Huh." An idea was starting to take shape in my mind, like a distant speck on the horizon. "You have other songs too?"

"I've got one about renewable biofuels." He shrugged. "Ethanol, propanol."

"Wow," I said. <u>Ethanol</u> is a word you rarely heard in rap songs, and for good reason. "I'd like to hear it," I said.

"Yeah?" He disappeared behind a row of lockers, and came back with pants and a shirt on. He hopped on one foot, pulling on a sock. "I'm not sure if it's too, I don't know." He frowned. "Weird."

"Sing a few lines," I suggested.

He shrugged. "If you want."

I tried not to look eager.

"It starts out like ..." Ty nodded to an imaginary beat. He put on a rapper's scowl, and stuck his lower lip out.

"Mackin' on a fuel ... that's <u>renewable</u> C'mon, people ... it's way <u>do-able</u>!"

"Keep going," I said, without taking my eyes off him. "Take all the time you need."

CHAPTER SEVEN

"You guys are putting on a school talent show?" asked Morgan. The whole table was staring at Jasper and me. "How'd you come up with that?"

I couldn't tell her that after Ty's private rap concert I raced home to call Jasper.

An act that terrible _had_ to have a wider audience. I came up with the talent show idea, figuring we could kill two birds with one stone: raise money to renovate the playground, and get Ty to publically embarrass himself.

It was a win-win.

"The idea just — came to me." I coughed. "There's, like, so much talent at this school."

Silence.

"Yeah," agreed Jasper, after I kicked him under the table.

Actually, I thought just the opposite. The big dance number in the fall musical was so disorganized, it looked like a fire drill. Other

events, like the kick line in the Eighth Grade Dance-Off, were just as bad.

"Talent shows are great fund-raisers," I continued. "We can charge twenty dollars admission."

Everyone blasted us with questions.

"What's the date?"

"When are tryouts?"

"Where will it be?"

"Whoa, whoa, whoa." I held up my hands in front of my face, feeling totally overwhelmed. I wasn't prepared for their questions — or excitement. "We're still, uh, working out the details."

That was an understatement. We hadn't really gotten any further than "let's have a talent show" and "yeah!" A grinding feeling in my stomach told me we should have waited to announce this. But the thought of exposing Ty's rap skills was so exciting, I'd gotten carried away.

Suddenly, everyone was yelling out ideas.

"Maya makes shadow animals!"

"Cody does yo-yo tricks!"

"I could show my snow globe collection!"

Shadow animals? Snow globes?

    "Have you guys ever put on a show before?"
Morgan's eyes narrowed as she turned to me.
She was a big Drama Clubber. "I've never seen
you at play tryouts."

    "I was Third Tree on the Left in <u>The
Story of Photosynthesis</u>," offered Jasper.

    The table went silent again.

    I gulped. "We're not performers, we're more
like — producers."

    "What have you produced?" asked Kendra.

    "Um ..." I suddenly felt defeated. "Nothing,
really."

    "Our goal is to renovate the playground,"
Jasper reminded everyone. "And this seemed

optimal." I was grateful he jumped in, even
if he sounded like he was pitching life
insurance.

    "That's cool," said Kendra, and the girls
nodded.

    "When are auditions?"

    "Are there prizes?"

    "What about —"

I stood up before they could ask more questions, pulling Jasper by the collar of his sweater. Thinking about the amount of work ahead of us made my head spin. "We have to go," I told everyone.

"But I haven't finished..." he pointed to his chicken wrap.

"Production meeting!" I explained, dragging him away.

"Say what?" Mr. Amundson, our assistant principal, stroked his chin and frowned.

"A talent show." I shifted in my seat in his office.

"Talent show?" he asked. "I thought you were going to ask to use the color copier."

We looked around his office. There was a poster of an MTV show on the wall and a giant bowl of popcorn on his desk, all part of a campaign to show how cool and kid-friendly he was. We were there after school during an hour he usually advertised as "Kickin' It with the Assistant Principal."

S'up, dawgs?

   "It's — we want to raise money to renovate a playground." I tried to refocus. "For P.S. 160, a school in a poor neighborhood." I looked at Jasper, who nodded.

   "Okay, I'm down with that," Amundson said. "When? Where?"

   "In the auditorium next month —"

   "Next month!" he shouted. "You can't just have the school auditorium. You've got to, like, request it. You feel me?"

   "Okay." I shrugged. "We're requesting it now."

   "Dawgs, the auditorium's booked months in advance." Amundson took a handful of popcorn and leafed through his calendar. "The wood

Shop Awards, the Geography Bee, Math Family Fun Night..."

I could only imagine how crowded that would be.

"You better think about next year," said Amundson.

Next year! We had to jump on this thing, before Ty realized how terrible he was. We couldn't wait a year!

"Isn't there _one_ free night?" I begged.

"Plus, you'd need approval," Amundson said. "From the student council. Principal's office. PTA...."

Oh, God. This was getting more and more complicated.

"Can't we do it sooner?" Jasper asked. "Those kids would sure like a new playground."

"And I'd like a Jaguar Supersport," said Amundson. "But it ain't gonna happen. And neither is —"

The door cracked open behind us.

"Greetings," said a lordly voice.

Oh, no. It was Principal Kulbarsh. Without even thinking, I tucked in my shirt. Unlike Amundson, Principal Kulbarsh never tried to be cool. He moved down the hall like the King of England, rarely cracking a smile, eyes focused ahead in a Great Upward Stare.

* KULBARSH
AT-A-GLANCE

Pet peeves: Nose rings,
    bad grammar
Favorite word:
    "Tomfoolery"
Went bald at: 10

"What brings you here?" Kulbarsh turned his death-stare on Jasper and me. "Gentlemen?"

"We, uh, want to hold a school talent show," I stammered. My palms were sweating. "For a fund-raiser. To renovate a playground in a poor neighborhood."

Amundson broke in. "Normally, I'm all over charity gigs, but the auditorium's booked solid. We could shoot for next year. . . ."

"Mmmm. I see." Kulbarsh sat down on a chair next to us. "When did you want to do it?"

"Sometime next month," I said. "Sir."

"This show." Kulbarsh spoke slowly, squinting at the ceiling. "The performers would be students?"

"Yeah. Yes." I corrected myself. The room fell silent.

"Would there be room for . . ." Kulbarsh cleared his throat. "Faculty members?"

HUH?

Was it possible Principal Kulbarsh, the most stern, high-minded, unsmiling enemy-of-fun actually wanted to perform? It was so absurd, Jasper and I just looked at each other.

After a moment's adjustment, we nodded
frantically. "FOR SURE!" I sputtered. "Faculty
members! Definitely!"

"Glad to hear it." Kulbarsh stood up.
"Maurice, let me see the calendar." Amundson
handed it to him. "On the eighteenth of next
month, can't Chess for Success meet in the
Multi-Purpose Room?"

"What? I suppose —" Amundson looked flustered.
"But it would have to be approved by ..."

"It's a talent show," barked Kulbarsh. "Not
a moon launch. Make it happen!"

What? Did I hear him right? Jasper and I
looked at each other, amazed. Kulbarsh was
letting us do the talent show so he could perform?
It was so crazy I could hardly believe it.

Amundson started to protest, and then stopped.

"On it," he said glumly.

Woo-hoo!

My hand met Jasper's in a high five.

We stood up and walked out with the principal. None of us spoke. Before heading to his office, he turned to us. "Best of luck with the talent show."

We shook hands with him.

"Not many people know it," he said. "But I'm an enthusiastic yodeler."

I looked at Jasper. We were in for a wild ride.

* CHAPTER EIGHT *

We'd just finished watching the first set of auditions. I turned to Jasper.

If <u>everyone</u> was this bad, how was Ty going to stand out?

We were slumped in orange plastic chairs in the Multi-Purpose Room. That round of tryouts had started off with a sixth grader playing "We Will Rock You" on water glasses. Morgan did a dramatic reading from <u>Gossip Girl</u>. Someone else ate seven hot dogs in a row.

"Do we need more flyers?" I asked. "Maybe

word isn't getting out to the <u>really</u> talented."

And who <u>were</u> those really talented kids, anyway? Since we posted the flyer, it seemed like every kid in school had told us about their fantastic monologue from <u>High School Musical</u>,

> **FORD'S GOT TALENT!**
>
> Strut your stuff at
>
> Gerald Ford Middle School's Talent Night
>
> Tryouts Thursday and Friday 2:45 to 5:00
>
> Sign up today! We dare you!
>
> Produced by Danny Shine and Jasper Wozniak

or Justin Bieber tribute band. But the people we'd auditioned so far hadn't been too impressive.

I opened the door for the next audition. In came a petrified-looking girl in a white leotard.

"My name is Shawna Boyle? I'll be doing 'Waltz of the Snowflakes'? From The Nutcracker?"

Jasper and I nodded for her to start.

"One, two, three . . ." Shawna counted out loud.

Grunting, she hoisted herself up on pink toe shoes and lifted shaking arms above her head. After a couple of sluggish spins, she leaped and landed with a heavy thud. For a finale, she did a labored jump-kick, knocking over a metal garbage can.

So much for untapped talent at Gerald Ford Middle School.

We helped her clean up the garbage, and she started to whimper. "I blew it, right? I won't be in the show, will I?" I looked at Jasper helplessly. While watching her, my reaction had been, "not in a million years." But seeing her tear-streaked face, I realized it was going to be hard to say no.

In fact, how were we going to say no to anybody? We weren't anonymous talent scouts — we'd have to face the classmates we'd rejected all day, every day.

This was going to get sticky.

"We'll post the list Friday," I said. "Nice job!"

"This is pathetic," Jasper said to me after she had left. "Is there anyone talented at this school at all?"

I checked the list. Next up was Axl, my worst enemy.

Axl was the school bully I'd met in detention hall. I had drawn a tattoo of a flaming skull on Axl's arm with a Sharpie, which he treasured like an original Picasso. He showed his gratitude by putting me into a headlock every time he saw me.

Our big clash came when I'd brought him to my favorite store, Comix Nation. When I wasn't looking, he stole a collectible  comic book and framed me for the crime. After I got him in trouble, he had to work at the store for free. Ever since, he always looked like he was deciding whether or not to ice me.

Now he was walking into the audition room.

"Hey." Axl twisted my arm behind my back, his way of saying hello. "Spike and Boris are on their way. We've got a band."

Axl, Boris, and Spike made up the Skulls, Gerald Ford's only gang. For fun, they pulled fire alarms, set off cherry bombs in trash cans, and decorated lockers with shaving cream.

Their band was news to me.

A second later, Boris showed up in a black sweatshirt dotted with drops of electric orange nacho sauce. As the #2 Skull, he had a Cro-Magnon brow and rarely smiled. He walked in with

Spike, the school's scariest Korean bully. He liked to play with fire. The three of them got busy setting up their guitar, drum set, and keyboard.

"Your band is . . . ?" I said.

"MutilatoR," said Axl. "The song is called `Venom's Bloody Valentine."

Right.

"Let's do this!" Axl yelled. He dropped to his knees, glided across the floor like he was facing a stadium of pumping fists, and leaped to his feet. "GERALD FORD MIDDLE SCHOOLLLLL!" he yelled. "ARE YOU READY TO ROCK?"

Jasper and I looked at each other. Were we supposed to answer?

"I SAID," he roared, "ARE YOU READY TO ROCK?"

"Er, yes," I said uncertainly.

"SAY IT LOUDER!"

"Yes!"

"ALLLLRIGHT!" Axl screeched. "Let's do this!" Boris started drumming furiously. He wasn't too rhythmic, but he was noisy.

Axl nodded at the other guys, and they exploded into a blistering sonic rant that tore through the room like a heavy-metal tsunami.

He didn't so much play his guitar as attack it, hammering the same three chords over and over again.

And then he started to sing.

"Burning flesh torn from the bone
Toxic ashes flood the zone

Skinned alive in deadly rain
Gouged-out eyes cry out in pain

Die, spirit, die!
Now we . . . must . . . die."

His voice rang out in a sickly wail, cracking when he hit the high notes. Truthfully, he wasn't much of a singer, or guitar player. But he strutted around as if a laser show blazed behind him, and flames were licking at his feet. He owned the stage — or at least, the Multi-Purpose Room.

I was impressed. Who knew Axl had rock star aspirations? It made him more interesting. Just when I thought the intensity couldn't get any higher . . .

They took it up a notch.

"HYAHHHHHHHHHHHHH!"

Axl threw his guitar into the air. He caught it and pretended to play it upside down, then whipped it behind his back. He aimed it like a machine gun, and brought it low between his knees. Frantically imitating every guitar move imaginable, Axl wasn't deterred by lack of skill.

And it wasn't over.

Eyes blazing, Axl grabbed an orange chair, whipped it over his head, and brought it down like a sledgehammer. He hit the floor over and over, as if trying to smash it to smithereens.

"Unh." He grunted. "Unhhhh!"

Holy crud!

Axl started a crazy path of destruction through the room, throwing down chairs and overturning tables. Boris picked up a metal garbage can and rolled it into the wall. Spike jumped up and down on the keyboard, grinding the keys together in a deafening crash.

Jasper and I ducked.

"Freakin' A!" yelled Boris.

POUND! POUND! POUND!

Through the glass panel in the door, I saw a very angry Mrs. Lacewell.

"What the <u>blazes</u>?" she burst out when I let her in. She was the school administrator and ran GFMS like a military base. Looking around, I could see  why she was upset. The place looked like Ozzy Osbourne's hotel room after a rough night.

"Talent show auditions," I explained. Axl and the guys started picking up chairs.

"By who — Godzilla?" she demanded. "I want this room cleaned up ASAP. With the water cooler rightside up." She turned to Jasper and me. "You two are responsible for any damage."

When the door shut behind her, Axl came over and slapped Jasper and me on the shoulders. "Sorry Lacewell went crazy. But never mind her." Axl drew our heads together for a cozy chat. "What'd you guys think?"

"Um —"

"Obviously, it'll be better with more amps."

I tried to imagine the sound being louder.

"Look." I had to word this right. "I was really with it, until the end. But you can't, like, throw chairs and stuff."

"That's part of the act!" Axl protested.

"He didn't set his guitar on fire," Boris pointed out.

"Or eat a live bat," Spike added.

"You heard Lacewell," Jasper said. "If school property gets damaged, we're responsible."

"But that was _nothing_!" Axl's voice rose. "You ever seen Cult of Napalm? Or Internal Bleeding?"

"They're not in seventh grade," I sighed.

The truth was, I'd rather have them than some lame baton twirler. But what kind of damage would they do to the auditorium?

I tried flattery. "You guys need a bigger venue. Someplace with stadium seating and a JumboTron."

"I know." Axl's voice got husky. "I KNOW!"

"That'd be a better place for your —"

"Thing is, though." Axl leaned in. "We _need_ this gig. We've got to promote Goblet of Doom."

"Goblet . . ."

"Our new CD." He grabbed a hunk of my T-shirt and twisted it until my chest started to burn. "You _have_ to take us. Saying no isn't really, like . . ." He tightened his grip. "An option."

Suddenly I couldn't breathe.

"Turn us down, and —" POUND! POUND! POUND! People outside were knocking on the door.

"You're _dead_," Axl said sweetly.

He released me, and I fell back, coughing. "Other auditions —" I choked out, as I stumbled toward the door.

"You'll make the right decision." Axl slapped my back again as his crew headed out.

I looked at my clipboard, and mopped my forehead.

Only 23 people left to see.

* CHAPTER NINE *

"What a disaster," I moaned.

We'd been watching America's Least Talented for three straight hours, and we were bleary, limp, and exhausted.

"The hula-hoopist," I whined. "The fortune-teller. The girl who collects seashells. The —"

"First-aid demonstration." Jasper's voice was dead.

"Oh, God." Where were all the really exciting acts?

"Well, it's too late to bail now. Next up..." Jasper checked the clipboard. "Chantal."

Chantal?

That was interesting. She was supposed to be a good singer, but I'd never seen her perform. What if we had to reject her? The most Axl could do was kill us. Chantal was capable of much, much worse.

In five minutes, she could destroy our reputations, and make everyone at school stop talking to us. People she didn't like became radioactive and stayed that way. The damage was irreversible.

POUND! POUND! POUND! I saw Chantal's coiled hairdo through the door window.

"Danny Shine!" she yelled. "Move those chicken legs and let me in!"

I opened the door reluctantly. She strolled in like a queen, wearing a shiny black trench coat. An entourage of girls in

matching outfits swarmed in behind her. And behind them, two slim guys in warm-up suits.

"This is where we're auditioning?" Chantal frowned. She'd been here for five seconds, and she was already complaining.

"Take it or leave it." I tried to sound tough.

We watched in amazement as someone wheeled in a large spotlight. One girl set up an iPod dock in the corner, while someone else plugged in a light that projected a giant "C" onto the wall behind her.

Everyone spread out and took their place on the floor. Chantal dropped her head dramatically, and one of the guys introduced her.

"I'd like to present Chantal and Her Sophisticated Ladies," he said smoothly. "No videotaping — please!"

I rolled my eyes.

"One, two . . . one-two-three!"

Chantal's head snapped up, and she whipped off her shiny trench coat. Underneath was a gold-sequined top and black leggings. Irresistible dance beats filled the room, and Chantal started gliding, strutting, and sashaying to the music. Behind her, the girls shimmied and writhed.

"Get live, Lady Bling. Lady Bling, get live!" The dancers chanted.

Jasper and I bolted upright.

"How y'all doing tonight?" Chantal purred. "I'm Lady Bling, Divine Miss Thing, Goddess of the Hottest, and Stoked to Sing. I'm rated ten, have tons of friends, got it goin' on like a hot pink Benz."

The dancers fanned out, and the boys started doing aerials and cartwheels. Then she started belting.

"I'm a diva I'm told
With jewels ice-cold
My underwear is
Solid gold."

    I was used to Chantal having a stadium-sized personality. The thing was... Chantal could also sing!
    Her power anthem rocked the room. As she piled on the beats, boy dancers flanked her with kicks and occasional flips. They lifted Chantal up so high, I thought she'd bust through the ceiling.
    Then the girl dancers hit the floor with glowing neon jump ropes, and Chantal dove in. For five minutes, she blew us away

with the speediest, sassiest double-Dutch moves ever.

Jasper's mouth was open too. After watching every two-bit kazoo player at school, this was halftime at the Super Bowl.

"I'm a triple threat, and doing it greatly
So freakin' hot
I wish I could date me."

Her brags were so outrageous, you had to laugh. But her singing and dancing were the real deal. My eyes met Jasper's and we nodded excitedly. This was it — the act that could save the show!

We stood up and clapped like crazy.

"You've been a great audience," Chantal cooed. She blew us a kiss. "Good night!"

The group took an elaborate bow, and then high-fived each other. I ran up to Chantal. "That was awesome!"

"Thanks," she said coolly, checking her makeup in a pocket mirror. She snapped

her mirror shut and called out to one of the guys in warm-up suits. "Hello!" she yelled. "Hair gel!"

A Warm-Up Suit Guy ran over.

"You're a really good dancer," I said. "And singer and . . . jump ropist." Was that the right term? She calmly rubbed styling goop into her hair. "You're in!"

This was her chance to jump up and down, and squeal, "Thanks, Danny! That's so great!"

Instead, she shrugged. "If you want to make an offer, talk to my agent."

Jasper and I looked at each other.

Agent?

She opened the door, and in walked Phil Petrokis. Now I was confused. What was my computer lab partner doing here?

"Hey, Danny." He handed me a card.

PHIL PETROKIS

Managing Talent Since 6th Grade

"The sky's the limit!"

"I handle all her bookings," he said.

"It's not a booking!" Jasper protested.

Phil took out a buttery leather briefcase.

"Here's her contract," he said. "Standard boilerplate."

I grabbed it and started reading. Stuff about event cancellation, TV coverage, rehearsal time. Okay, I could cope with that. Then, at the bottom, a line jumped out.

"Private dressing room?" I read out loud. "Fridge stocked with diet root beer and Jolly Ranchers?"

Jasper plucked it out of my hand. "Let me see that."

"Got to take this call." Petrokis walked away with his phone. In the corner we heard him yelling. "No way," he said. "Ten percent of the gross, or she's out!"

I kept reading. "Bowls of M&M's with no green ones?"

"Routine stuff." Phil whispered, covering his phone.

"Extra security!?" Jasper read. "Hair and makeup person?"

"Very basic," said Phil.

"Phil." I gritted my teeth. "Do you realize this is a <u>middle school talent show</u>? We can't cater to every student. As it is, we can barely —"

Phil folded up his phone. "Chantal is very hot right now," he said. "I've got big plans for her: TV show, record deal, skin care line . . ."

"Yeah, but —"

"She's got interest from other gigs," Phil continued. "The Spring Concert, Teen Stunt Night, Green-a-palooza —"

Green-a-palooza?

Jasper and I gasped. No way could we lose our best act to Ty's show!

"Let's go, Phil." Chantal sounded disgusted. "I talked to the other kids auditioning. I don't belong with seashell collectors and first-aid demonstrators. That's beneath me."

"NO!" I pleaded.

"Too bad," Chantal said. "'Cuz I was hoping to get my friend T-Bone to do the show. He does old-school break-dancing. . . ."

What? That sounded great.

"And my girl Raina. She does kickin' skateboard stunts. . . ."

Huh? Where were these people?

"But they won't do it unless I give a thumbs-up." Chantal gathered up a duffel bag covered with buckles and gold chains. "And

apparently you guys just aren't serious about getting real entertainment."

"Yes, we are!" My voice was desperate. "We can work something out." I looked at Jasper, who was nodding furiously. "Hershey's Bars, M&M's, limo rides. Whatever you want!"

"Yeah?" Chantal stuck her chin out. "'Cuz I might want a few more things. . . ."

"Like what?"

"Fridge stocked with VitaminWater, Cheez Curls, and organic snow cones?"

"You got it."

"Cheez Curls have to be Ragin' Cajun."

"Right."

"Limo to pick me up?"

"Check."

"Extra security for hard-to-handle fans?"

"Er . . . check."

"How about pyrotechnics?" she asked.

"We'll see what's possible," I said, as Jasper poked me.

At that point, I would have agreed to a helicopter with built-in hot tub. We just needed her in the show. As for her demands? We'd just have to make some substitutions.

* OUTRAGEOUS DEMAND
CONVERSION CHART

"Private dressing room" = janitor's closet

"Extra security" = a hall monitor

"Stretch limo" = Jasper's Razor scooter

"Stocked fridge" = candy bar

"Hot tub" = kids' pool
"Pyrotechnics" = guy with flashlight

Phil came up and slapped us on the back. "Glad we could work something out." I nodded at Jasper, dazed. I turned to Chantal. "Tell your friends to stop by for auditions tomorrow."

"I will," said Chantal. "See you at dress rehearsal. And make sure you have decent snacks there. Sushi, mini-egg rolls, whatever."

Snacks for rehearsal? I walked away, wondering what I had gotten myself into.

* CHAPTER TEN *

With Chantal & Company on board, the talent show went from optional to Must-See. Suddenly everyone was buzzing about it, and stopping Jasper and me in the hall. "Is Pinky Shroeder really doing karaoke-juggling?" they'd ask. For the first time in school, I felt . . .

Un-invisible.

So when a bunch of girls called out to me during gym, I knew it was about The Big Event. Both guys and girls were having phys ed outdoors, and people were milling around the track, waiting for their teacher to blow the whistle.

"Hey, Danny!" Kendra waved me over. "We have to ask you something."

I walked over casually, like a bunch of girls calling my name out was no big deal. The girls looked so excited, I wondered what this was about. Rehearsals? Costumes? Auditions?

"Hey there." I used my deep Talent Show Director voice.

"Just wondering." Sophie tugged at my sleeve. "Are you drawing the poster for Green-a-palooza?"

My smile froze. Why were we talking about Ty's show?

"No one asked me." I shrugged, but I felt my confidence drop.

"That's weird," Emma said. "I mean, you draw everything else." Glad she noticed. I was always making posters for <u>some</u> lame event.

Why hadn't Ty asked me? He probably thought I wasn't cool enough.

Yeah. That was it.

"Maybe the poster'll have Skye Blue on it," Sophie buzzed. "Oooh!"

"Skye Blue?" I was confused. He was a famous stunt bicyclist. Everyone had seen the YouTube video that had made the 22-year-old instantly famous. Now he was such a big star, he had his own video game.

"Duh," said Morgan. "Haven't you heard? He's the headliner at Green-a-palooza!"

WHAT???

Ty had gotten Skye Blue for Green-a-palooza!?

"He's a friend of Ty's dad," said Morgan, answering my next question.

My chest burned, thinking how unfair it was. Because of his dad's contacts, Ty had lucked out.

TWEEEEEEEEEEEEEEEEEEW!

The ear-piercing screech of Coach Kilshaw's whistle made me jump.

"Hey, Shine!" he roared. "Are you in the girls' class now?"

"Maybe he has his period!" yelled Axl, and all the guys snickered.

I hurried away from the girls and joined a ragged group jogging around the track.

I couldn't stop thinking about Skye Blue. He was the <u>definition</u> of cool — a butt-kickin' bike stunt rider known for signature moves like the Leap of Death and Jedi Knight.

No one was more popular than Skye. Jasper

and I had seen him on our favorite show, Extreme Bike Smackdown.

Oh, man!

Just as the talent show was getting a tailwind, Green-a-palooza had to come along  and blow it out of the water! No WAY could we compete with Skye Blue.

It had never even occurred to me to worry about Green-a-palooza stealing our thunder; I was picturing a snoozefest packed with nature lectures and recycling demonstrations.

<u>Not</u> the hottest ticket in town!

"What's a matter, Shine?" Coach "Twenty Laps" Kilshaw pulled up beside me. "Pick up the pace."

"Unh," I grunted, trying to sprint away from him.

Ahead of me, two jocks were talking.

"...see the video of him doing stunts at the Grand Canyon?" said a big-necked guy. "It was sweet."

<u>Everyone</u> was talking about Skye!

Now Green-a-palooza would be bigger than ever. I cursed Ty under my breath, wondering how he'd managed to upstage us again.

"ARE YOU FREAKIN' KIDDING ME?"

Jasper didn't take the news well. "How did he get the coolest bike stuntman _ever_?" He shook his head. "Green-a-palooza gets Skye Blue, and we get" —
Jasper looked at the clipboard —
"Principal Kulbarsh. Yodeling."

We were in Ralph the janitor's closet, sitting on boxes of supplies, eating Twizzlers and taking care of business.

"Ty's dad knows him," I said. "But don't freak out. We've got Chantal! And cool acts like the skateboarder/breakdancer. And even if Green-a-palooza's a hit, Ty's _still_ going to embarrass himself at the talent show." I smiled, remembering his eco-rap in the bathroom.

"You know, Danny." Jasper's voice was low. "It just hit me. Ty didn't audition. I hope he's still up for this."

Crud. Jasper was right.

"Did he even sign up to try out?" I scanned the list. Ty's name wasn't there. "Oh, no. He's our whole —"

"Reason for doing this." Jasper's face turned white.

"He's got to be in the show." My heart was pounding. How did this happen?

"Find him ASAP," Jasper said. "Make sure he's on board —"

"But —" School was almost over. "What do I do if . . . ?"

"Promise him anything," said Jasper.

"Um —"

"Ahem." We looked up. Ralph the janitor was standing over us with a mop. The meeting was over.

I looked for Ty at his locker, but he was gone. Some girl said he was at the Lakeside Bird

Sanctuary. I rolled my eyes. Why couldn't he do normal things after school like the rest of us?

    The shelter was a modern stone and glass building at the edge of a nature preserve. I found Ty in a huge room that looked like an indoor zoo. Birds were flying around everywhere.

Ty was cradling a wounded bird and feeding it through a tiny eyedropper.

"Danny!" He looked surprised to see me. "Are you a Youth Service Leader too?"

"No," I said sheepishly. Even when he didn't mean to, Ty always made me feel not-quite-good-enough. "What are you doing?" I asked, pointing to the eyedropper. I ducked to avoid flying birds.

"I'm feeding Tango," he explained. "He's a hybrid macaw, left homeless after the flood downstate. This is an animal rescue unit. We take wounded birds and rehabilitate them. Say hi to Danny," Ty said to the feathery bundle.

"Um, hi, Tango," I muttered. What do you say to a bird?

"I also help microchip new ones when they come in." He put the macaw down, and showed me its ankle bracelet. "It's not bad. On my last  Service gig, I had to test the water quality of the drainage canal. This is better."

THUMP! A red bird hit the table next to us  like a B-1 bomber. I jumped back, startled. It began pecking a cloth-covered book, and Ty gently shooed him away. "Yours?" I asked, picking it up. I loved looking at people's notebooks.

"Yeah, it's mine," Ty said. "I'm journaling while I do this."

Of course.

"So, if you're not volunteering," Ty said, "what are you doing here?"

"Oh. Right." My urgent mission suddenly felt a little stupid. Couldn't I have waited until school tomorrow? "Jasper and I are putting together the talent show for Saturday night, the eighteenth, and we really want you to be in it." I took a deep breath. "You're going to do your eco-rap, right?"

"My eco-rap." Ty narrowed his eyes. "H-m-m-m-m."

K-KAW! K-KAW! A yellow bird sailed by. I was sure the next low-flying one was going to bonk me.

"You remember." My voice went higher.

"It's a fund-raiser to renovate that children's playground in the city. At P.S. 160."

"Yeaahh," he said slowly, rubbing his chin. "Problem is, I'm busy doing this thing Mondays and Wednesdays. Tuesdays I have Save The Oceans, Saturday's soccer. Plus I'm totally jammed with Green-a-palooza. That reminds me . . ."

"But . . . !"

Crud. Crud. Crud.

"Can you draw the Green-a-palooza poster?" Ty asked. "I meant to ask you earlier. . . ."

"Um, well —"

"Sorry I have to bail on the talent show," Ty said. "But there's so much to do for Green-a-palooza! Setting up a website and ticket sales. Working with the stage crew for tech rehearsals. Printing up a program. Getting donations to cover the costs of the show. Access for the handicapped. Ads in local papers to get the word out — and so on. But I don't have to tell you about all that!"

Sheesh.

Listening to him, my stomach sank like a

stone. We hadn't thought about any of those things. And our show was two weeks before his!

YIPES.

Right now, though, my big job was to change Ty's mind. My palms started to sweat. I grabbed his shoulders.

"Ty, listen to me." My voice was deadly serious. "You've GOT to perform. It's really, really important. You need to get —" I locked eyes with him. "Your ecological message out there!"

I made a sweeping hand gesture and hit a bird station, causing a flutter of wings behind me.

Ty stared at me. "Wow, Danny," he said quietly. "I had no idea you felt so strongly about the environment."

I looked at the ground and blinked.

"This is a whole new side of you," he continued. "It's cool. I respect it. About the talent show —" Ty bit his lip. "I've never rapped before in public."

"There's a first time for everything," I pointed out.

"I don't know." Ty shook his head. "Tell you what. I'll do your show, if you'll draw the Green-a-palooza poster."

"That sounds —"

SPLAT!

A green bird came out of nowhere, pelting my head like a crop duster.

"— awesome," I said, wiping away the poop.

CHAPTER ELEVEN

Now that we had Ty on board, we could announce the performers. That night, Jasper posted the results online. The fallout didn't come until the next day, when I got to my locker.

"Guess Axl saw the posting." I bit my lip.

We knew there would be trouble if we nixed his heavy-metal act. But what could we do? We couldn't have Axl & Co. smashing furniture onstage.

In case we'd missed the words on our

lockers, he left other messages at school. The cement wall outside the gym said, DANNY REEKS and HEAVY METAL RULES, NOT SHORT UGLY GEEKS. They also marked up my poster for the show:

Axl's reaction was the most extreme, but there were tough moments with other people too. Katelyn Ogleby gave me a tearful look for rejecting her twirling glow stick dance.

"I'm really sorry," I said. "We had a limited number of spots." I felt like a rat having to say no to anyone. But the important thing was to get Ty up there, doing what he did worst.

We needed an emcee for the show. It hadn't occurred to me until Ty mentioned it in his to-do list. But of course, an announcer had to greet the audience, introduce guests, say stuff between acts, and stop people who went on too long.

"You do it," said Jasper. "Or I'll do it."

Jasper was perfectly comfortable with a three-minute silence in the middle of a conversation. He used phrases like, "Egads!" and "suboptimal." His emcee style was only right for certain events.

And me? <u>Not</u> a good idea. I freeze in front of an audience like a deer in headlights. Once I had to give an oral report on "Traditions of the Hopi Indians," and I forgot some basic things, like how to speak and breathe.

Other than that, it went great.

So who could we get? I tried to think of someone who was funny, but also mature, and comfortable with a crowd. Pickings were pretty slim. Funny and mature don't really go together in middle school.

"Do you have an emcee yet?" Someone was tapping me on the shoulder. It was Malibu Nussbaum. "I've had a lot of public speaking experience." She must have overheard us arguing about it.

Hmmm. Malibu was a student council type, always campaigning for Healthier Cafeteria Meals or No School Budget Cuts. Had I ever heard her say anything funny? If so, I couldn't remember it.

"Thanks for asking, Malibu," I said. "Just curious. What other shows have you emceed?"

"The Recycling Assembly," she said. "The Teacher Appreciation Breakfast. The Student Council Awards."

What a line-up.

"The important thing is, emcees need to show respect for other students," Malibu continued earnestly.

I frowned. "Respect" isn't a word that goes with comedy. I thanked her and said we'd let her know. Back at the "office," I talked it over with Jasper.

"Malibu's not a good fit," I told him. "But who is? I can't think of a student or faculty member who's entertaining in the right way."

We heard a bucket sloshing down the hall, and the metal door opened.

"RALPH!" we both shouted at the same time.

It hit me like a thunderbolt: Ralph would be the perfect emcee. Most janitors aren't known for their public speaking skills, but Ralph was different. He was an actor!

He told us he'd only become a janitor to support himself between gigs. His real dream was to get a part on a TV show as a goofy dad or wisecracking best friend. He was always wondering if he should move to Los Angeles.

"G'day mates," Ralph said in an Australian accent. He liked to practice accents in case of movie auditions. We watched him wheel his bucket into the corner.

While he squeezed out his mop, I whispered to Jasper. "Are you thinking what I'm thinking?" I asked. "Let's ask Ralph to emcee!"

"Another Vulcan mind-meld." Jasper dapped me.

"Hey, guys," Ralph sat down on a drum of disinfectant. "Want to run lines with me?" He pulled a script out of his pocket.

"Sure." I shrugged. "What's the part?"

"Guy in a laxative commercial," he said. "You're my wife."

I took the script and located my first line.

"What's the matter, honey?" I put on a high, girlish voice.

"Constipation," Ralph said glumly. "And it's the day of the big Johnson presentation!"

I pressed a Sprite can into his hand. "Bowel-Ade relieves constipation fast. And it comes in a delicious mango flavor —"

"Skip to eight hours later," Ralph directed.

I turned the page. "How'd your day go?"

"No constipation," Ralph said proudly. "And we won the Johnson account!"

"Ewwww!" I had just read ahead in the script. "No way I'm kissing you."

Ralph laughed and we bumped fists instead.

"Good work," he said. "But I'll never get it.

"Well," I said, seizing the opening. "We've got a part for you. Want to emcee our talent show in a few weeks?"

"Wow," Ralph said. "What would I do?"

"Introduce people, banter between acts," I said. "Like the host at the Oscars."

"Cool," Ralph said. "That sounds fun. I'm flattered."

"We couldn't afford to pay you," Jasper said. "But you'd be doing us a big favor."

"It's about time people saw another side of you," I said. "Not just the guy mopping up barf after a basketball game."

"Emcee of the talent show," Ralph repeated dreamily. "I like it."

"Our people will call your people," I said, standing up.

"Wunderbar," said Ralph in a German accent.

"A JANITOR is emceeing the talent show?" shouted Amundson. "That's whack!"

The assistant principal was standing up in his office, practically yelling at Jasper and me. At first, I had questions about using Ralph too. He wasn't a very hard worker, and could be pretty self-absorbed. But Amundson's shouting instantly wiped my doubts away. Any idea he hated that much _had_ to be brilliant.

"Ralph studied acting at the Royal Shakespeare Academy of Milwaukee," I said calmly. "He's a member of the Screen Actors Guild, the Ventriloquists Union, and Pantomimes for Peace. He can tap-dance, sword fight, and impersonate Elvis. He's just what we need."

"What you _need_ is a faculty advisor." Amundson sat down. "This whole thing has gotten out of hand. Next you'll be saying you want to set off fireworks!"

Jasper and I stole a guilty look at each other, remembering Chantal's request for "pyrotechnics."

"So I'm assigning you someone you can kick it with, a member of the faculty who's down with your ideas. Someone who can say 'yay' or 'no way.' And that person will be . . ." He tapped on the desk dramatically with his pen.

"Me," he finished.

I almost fell over. Work with Amundson? I couldn't imagine anything worse.

Jasper and I both started sputtering.

"Um, really, we —"

"That's not —"

"Dawgs, it's settled." Amundson got up. "From now on, we meet every few days to see how things roll. This should have been done <u>weeks</u> ago. My bad."

What a low blow. He knew less about putting on a show than we did! Plus he was a complete doofus! On the other hand, he could be a useful testing board. Anything he liked — we'd do the opposite.

Using my new Talent Show Director skills, I smiled and said we'd be in touch.

* CHAPTER TWELVE *

We steered clear of Amundson, but it didn't take long for us to realize we needed other kinds of help — <u>big time</u>. So I put up flyers all over school:

TALENT SHOW VOLUNTEERS NEEDED!!!

Coat check!

Website!

Ticket Sales!

Parking!

Security!

See Danny or Jasper ASAP

I had a secret agenda: getting Asia O'Neill to volunteer by making <u>sure</u> she saw the poster right outside her homeroom. Instead of going to lunch, I snuck into the hall to find the bulletin board next to Room 209.

Too bad it was already crammed with flyers.

I rearranged the board to make room for our poster. Now Asia wouldn't miss it. Maybe she'd come up to me at lunch. "Hey, Danny," she'd say. "Do you still need people for stage crew?" And I'd say, "Sure. I think we could fit you in." And then she'd say . . .

WHOMP!

A thud on my shoulder jolted me out of my daydream.

"Nice poster," said a lazy voice.

Spinning around, I saw Axl, Boris, and Spike grinning. Boris was swinging a bicycle chain. Axl had his arms folded, looking at me through slitted eyes. Spike was grinding his teeth.

"Just the guy I was looking for." Axl's eyes glittered. "Let's take a walk."

Oh, crud.

Like I didn't know what that meant! The last time I'd taken a "walk" with Axl, Boris held me down while Axl started to pound me. It was the worst hour of my whole life. Should I yell? Maybe someone down the hall would hear.

"But —" I sputtered.

"Someplace private," Axl said. "Where we can talk."

Right.

We headed for the stairwell, their favorite

hangout. It was a good place to pelt people with ketchup-filled water balloons.

As the door shut, Axl flashed me an evil smile. "Now we can take care of business."

* AXL-TO-ENGLISH DICTIONARY

"Take a walk" = Maim beyond recognition
"Private" = Where I can beat you up
"Talk" = Fight
"Take care of business" = Punch your lights out

Boris glanced at the small window covered in mesh. "Want me to stand lookout?" he asked Axl.

"No." Axl shook his head and kept walking. "We're not staying. We're taking him down to the boiler room."

The boiler room?

That was like a medieval torture chamber! Steam poured from the pipes, and greenish slime oozed over cement floors. There were window bars, like a prison. Maybe even rats. My body wouldn't be found for days. . . .

Double crud.

I followed Axl down the stairs, with Spike and Boris close behind. Why had I ignored their graffiti? Why hadn't I gotten Lacewell or another adult to explain the audition results to them? Why had I waited for the inevitable day they'd find me alone and . . .

CRAAAAAAAAACK.

A door opened on the floor below — a stroke of luck! Looking down, I saw the pale, bald head of Mr. Gordimer, the puffy-faced wood shop teacher.

He couldn't control a class to save his life, but — any adult was better than none. In his usual fog, would he see me being led on a death march by the school's worst bullies?

Of course not.

We looked like a bunch of friends, hanging out. For a crazy moment, I thought of bursting out, "HELP! I'm being kidnapped!"

"Danny." Gordimer nodded, huffing as he climbed. "Norris, Boris, Spike." He stopped and wiped his forehead with a sleeve. "May I see your hall pass?"

YES!

Now we'd all get in trouble, including me —

but at least my life wouldn't end in the school boiler room. I looked at Axl, expecting him to back off. But he just whistled and stuffed his hand in his pocket.

Against all odds, he pulled out a yellow hall pass.

Gordimer squinted at it. "I don't have my glasses," he said finally, handing it back. Looking down, I saw the fakest forged hall pass in the history of middle school:

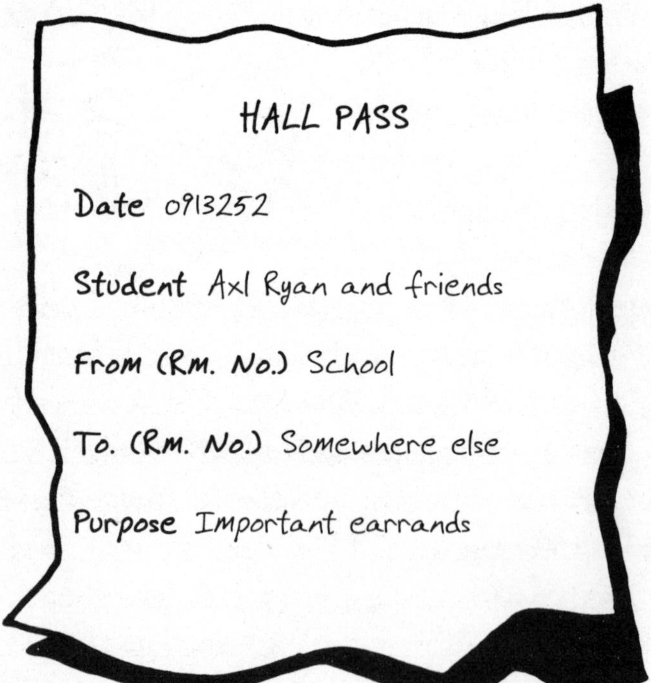

HALL PASS

Date 0913252

Student Axl Ryan and friends

From (Rm. No.) School

To. (Rm. No.) Somewhere else

Purpose Important earrands

Oh, man. Could this be more of a joke?

But Gordimer just shrugged and said, "Okay, fellows." Probably all he wanted was to get back to his newspaper. Even teachers didn't want to deal with these guys. He started to resume his climb up the stairs.

"Uh, Mr. Gordimer!" I blurted out, as he pulled away. Axl, Boris, and Spike looked at me sharply. When he turned to me, I chickened out. "Do you know what's for lunch?" I asked meekly.

"Pizza pockets." Gordimer sighed. "See you later, boys."

Axl poked me to keep moving. Finally, we hit the basement. The big metal door probably made this place soundproof — no wonder they brought victims there.

Now there was _no_ escape.

Boris pushed the door open, and steam poured out. Dodging the plume, they led me to a dank corner. Next to us, the giant boiler belched and hissed. It had to be at least a hundred degrees.

And I was sweating _before_ I got there.

Axl took a wire out of his backpack and slowly wound it around his arm. Was that some torture instrument? He seemed to be testing its sharpness.

"Yeah," he said. "This is _perfect_."

Oh, no. No, no, no, no.

He took the wire and walked toward me, pulling it taut. Boris and Spike nodded. Was this really happening? I closed my eyes and felt myself blink back hot tears.

"About this talent show . . ." Axl said.

Kill me! Just get it over with!

"We ARE going to be part of it. That's why we're going to —"

He pulled the wire tight.

"— work security."

HUH?

I opened my eyes. Axl moved past me and

looped the wire around the window handle. He
pried it open, and a blast of cool air poured in.

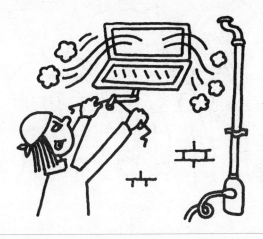

"Ahhh." He stuck his face into the breeze.

"You —" I sputtered. "Y-You're not going to
kill me?"

"Kill you?" Axl looked at me, surprised. "No."

I heaved a huge sigh.

"You thought we were gonna waste you?"
asked Boris. He turned to Spike. "He thought we
were gonna waste him!"

"Well —" It's not like it was <u>so</u> far-fetched.
"I knew you were mad about not getting into
the talent show —"

"I <u>was</u>, but —" Axl shook his head. "Not now.
That's in the past."

Like, this morning? The words on my locker looked freshly painted. "How about all that graffiti?" I asked.

"I told Boris and Spike to cut it out." Axl shrugged. "They didn't realize I was, like, over it."

Sheesh. "What made you change your mind?"

"Well..." Axl crouched down near one of the hissing pipes, and motioned for Boris, Spike, and me to join him. I pulled up a cardboard box. Axl's eyes got misty and philosophical. I'd seen this mode before, like the time he gave the "It's Every Guy's Dream to be a Skull" speech.

"I read this interview with Killa Whale." Axl was a huge Killa Whale fan, of course. "He says he always respects the promoter's vision." His voice rose. "If a venue isn't right, he won't perform there."

"So —"

"To do our show right, we need an arena. State of the art, with skyboxes and good sight lines. Not a dinky stage with four lights where you can't even throw a chair —"

"Or set a shirt on fire," added Spike.

"Uh-huh," I nodded. "I totally get that."
PHEW!

What a huge relief to have him off my back! But then I remembered what he did want. "So . . . ?"

"When I saw your poster," Axl said. "I realized we could help. You need a security team and we . . ." He pointed at Boris and Spike. "Do security."

But — Axl was someone you needed protection from!

I took a deep breath.

"About security." I jangled keys in my pocket, trying to avoid Axl's steel blue eyes. "Thanks for the offer, but — we're thinking of, uh, dealing with that ourselves."

"Deal with that yourselves?!" Axl snorted. "Are you KIDDING me? You guys couldn't beat up a third grader. The Skulls can help you out. Roam the halls. Punish people."

Wasn't that pretty much what they did every day?

"Um —"

"We could do pat downs." Axl's face lit up. "Like at the airport."

Hard to see what could go wrong with that scenario.

"Ask about uniforms," prodded Boris.

"Guys —"

"Would we wear badges?" Axl sounded excited. "Army gear?"

"How 'bout weapons?" asked Boris.

"Whoa, whoa!" I held my hand up. "This isn't Delta Force. You'd just be making sure people stay within the roped-off area. That's it! No physical contact! NO WEAPONS!"

"Not even Super Soakers for crowd control?" asked Spike.

"No!" I said.

But an idea was slowly swirling around in my head. Maybe having Axl's gang doing security wasn't such a bad idea. That way, they wouldn't cause trouble at the talent show, and they'd stop marking up my posters. As the saying goes, "Keep your friends close, and your enemies closer."

"It's okay." Axl reassured Boris and Spike. "If Danny says 'no weapons,' that's cool. Whatever he wants." He turned to me. "Well?"

"Okay," I said uncertainly. "Let's try it."

"Woo-HOO!" Axl, Spike, and Boris high-fived. RIIIIIIIIIIIIIIIIIIIIIIIIIIIING!!!!!!

The bell was actually louder in the boiler room and it made us all jump. "Can you guys meet me and our advisor after school for a planning meeting?" I asked.

"Can't," said Axl. "You know where we'll be."

I suddenly remembered. "Okay, we'll keep you posted." I held my hand up. "Bye."

Walking away, I had to laugh. We had the only security team in history serving detention.

* CHAPTER THIRTEEN *

Dress rehearsal was in 20 minutes.

Performers were trickling in, lacing up ballet shoes, shaking tambourines, testing yo-yos. Jasper and I were running around frantically, greeting people and trying to act like we had things under control.

"Hey, Danny." Ty waved.

"Hey, Ty." I walked past him quickly, avoiding eye contact. Tonight, the whole school would see his terrible rap act. Did I still have the nerve to send him out there?

"Danny." Jasper looked around and frowned. "Where's the stage crew?"

I shrugged. "Backstage, maybe?"

"They're not there."

"Really?" That was weird. "They know dress rehearsal starts at two, and the show's tonight." The stage crew guys were hard-core tech nerds who played laser tag and argued about the right viewing order of Star Wars movies.

Pinky Shroeder walked by, juggling. "They're at the mall seeing <u>Ice Tomb</u>."

Jasper grabbed Pinky. "What?"

"The 3D avalanche movie." Pinky squirmed out of Jasper's grip, still juggling. "Director's cut."

I pulled Jasper up the aisle to the back of the auditorium. "Do you know how to work this thing?" I asked, pointing to the lighting board, which controlled all the onstage lights. "Please say yes."

"Nope."

We stared at all the levers and switches. Since it was Saturday, no one was at school but our performers and Mr. Robinson, the security guard. Our faculty advisor, Assistant Principal Amundson, was down the hall, but the tech guys always ran the board.

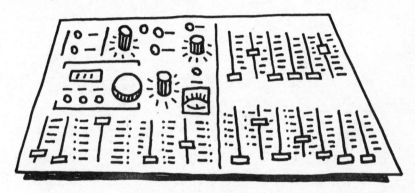

"It's like the control panel on the space shuttle," said Jasper. He moved a lever. A blue light came up on the corner of the stage.

"Can you figure it out?" I asked.

"Gimme three hours."

"How about ten minutes?"

There was a commotion at the double doors, and Chantal burst into the auditorium. Wearing sunglasses and a black cape with pink fur, she rolled in like a movie star.

Flanking her were 20 kids wheeling in luggage, props, and clothing racks.

"Danny. Jasper." Chantal came to a dramatic stop, halfway down the aisle.

She whipped off her cape. "Where's my dressing room?"

Crud!

In the rush of putting the show together I had completely forgotten our "contract" with Chantal. I tried to remember what insane things we'd promised her. . . .

We <u>had</u> to get her a dressing room. I tried to think of places at school we had access to. The Multi-Purpose Room? The Tech Center? Suddenly I had an idea. Fishing through Jasper's backpack, I pulled out a key. "Follow me, Chantal. You're going to like this."

She turned to Jasper. "Stephen will stay and explain my lighting concepts." Chantal pushed forward a slender boy in a warm-up suit. Then she and the rest of her army followed me up to the second floor, dragging garment bags and hair dryers.

When I stopped in front of Room 212, she froze.

"THE SCIENCE LAB?" Her voice was icy. "You've got to be kidding."

"It'll be good." I forced a smile. "Really!" I opened the door, and the smell of formaldehyde almost knocked us over.

"Ewwwwwwwww!" Chantal wrinkled her nose, and everyone groaned. "It smells like dead frogs. I can't get dressed in here. There's not even a full length mirror!"

"You can see your reflection in the storage closet. See?" I patted the steel door. The smell was kind of strong.

"That fridge better be stocked," she warned. "Diet root beer and Ragin' Cajun Cheez Curls."

"I'll check." The fridge was for chemicals, but sometimes Jasper hid snacks. I prayed this was one of those times. Blocking Chantal's view, I opened the door a crack. I peeked in. No soda, but —

A giant fetal pig.

Gross!

I whipped the door shut. "We ran out! No prob. I'll run over to Mighty Mart."

Chantal threw down a giant handbag. "You think when Beyoncé plays the Verizon Center, they run across the street?" She sounded genuinely hurt. "NO! Her pomegranate sparkling water's already chilling."

The crowd murmured "yeah" and "got that right."

"Two minutes," I said, running out the door.

I bolted down the stairs and out of the school. Sprinting across the lawn, I heard a shout from the window.

"Don't forget the M&M's!" yelled Chantal. "And — no green ones!"

"You went out for <u>chips</u>?" Jasper saw my grocery bag.

"They're not for me." I was panting. "It's Chantal! She —"

"Whatever." Jasper pulled some levers on the lighting board. "I've got to refocus these lights." Jasper headed off toward the wings. "You make an announcement. Say we're still working things out."

I ran up to the podium onstage, looking out on the endless rows of empty seats. In five hours, they'd be filled. What would it be like to stand here alone? All those people...

Looking at you. Waiting.

My knees felt shaky and a shiver ran up my neck. Thank God I wasn't performing.

"Hi." I cleared my throat. "I'm Danny. We're going to start rehearsal soon. We're just having a few little technical difficulties...."

"Like what?" A voice called out.

"Nothing important —"

CRAAAAAAAAAAAAAASH!

I looked behind me. A bulb had fallen and crashed to the floor.

"Sorry!" Jasper yelled from a ladder backstage.

The auditorium door opened and Amundson poked his head in. "Everything cool?"

"Great!" I said loudly.

THUD! A rope fell from the ceiling.

"Hold it, Danny." It was Ty. "Shouldn't we clear the stage before rehearsal starts?"

A tire rolled across a stage cluttered with junk. Having Ty point out the mess was embarrassing.

"Sorry!" Jasper's voice again.

"Also," Ty continued, "the lights look weird. What's up with that?"

I turned around. A light swirled crazily as

Jasper, up on a ladder, tried to re-aim it. "Oh, that? Jasper's, uh, trying out a new cross fade," I said. "Really cutting edge stuff."

"Hmmm." Ty sounded doubtful, and now other people were starting to look doubtful too. "Also wondering — where's the emcee?"

C'mon, Ty. Give it a rest.

"Ralph can't make it till tonight," I said. "Professional acting gig." No need to mention he was Freckles the Clown at a kid's birthday party.

Emboldened by Ty, other performers shouted: "Is it true the stage crew didn't show?" "Who's doing sound?" "Have you guys ever put on a show before?" I felt defeated. The performers had seemed happy enough until Ty started criticizing everything.

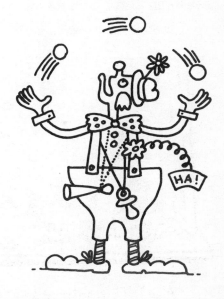

A rock tune began to play. Ty picked up his phone, and said loudly, "Hey, Skye! You got my message?" Then he put his hand over the phone, and announced importantly, "Sorry, it's Skye Blue. I have to take this."

He strutted out of the auditorium, cradling the phone on his shoulder.

"Uh-huh. Uh-huh. A 12 o'clock wheelie? Awesome."

Ooooooh. My dislike of him seemed to burn a hole in my chest. Wasn't it just like the guy, to flaunt his cool cred and his big star pal?

Well, that cool cred was about to disappear.

* CHAPTER FOURTEEN *

Half an hour later, things were moving right along.

Morgan's <u>Gossip Girl</u> reading wasn't nearly as bad as I'd feared. Kirby Hammer's "talent" — blowing a huge bubble out of bubble gum — held the crowd breathless. The Laff Riots, a couple of sixth graders, did a funny fake infomercial with squirt guns.

Confidence level: medium to good.

Rehearsal was moving at a fast clip. When they weren't performing,

everyone rushed back to their seats to watch the other acts. There was a good vibe as people clapped for each other. One girl was so happy after her gymnastic routine, she did a little dance.

Before this, the only thing I'd ever organized was a comic book trading session in someone's bedroom. I felt a flash of pride. Everyone is here today because of me and Jasper, I thought.

It was a pretty cool feeling.

Amundson slipped into the auditorium and sat down next to me. "This is dope," he whispered.

"Glad you like it." I looked down at the clipboard. Next up was Ty.

I gulped.

My feelings about Ty had gone back and forth. After his obnoxious phone call with Skye, I looked forward to him being humbled. But now that he was about to do it, I was strangely nervous for him.

Ty edged his way onto the stage uncertainly, looking small in the big, empty space. Pale beneath his soccer tan, he nodded for his music cue.

BOOM-DIDDA-BOOM. BOOM-DIDDA-BOOM...

The beats started, and Ty began nodding fiercely. "Uh-HUH," he grunted. Suddenly, his body started twitching back and forth, his thumbs pointing out. Was he dancing, or having a seizure?

Yipes! He was even <u>worse</u> than I remembered. Shakily, he blurted out:

"'Cuz I'm mean
I'm green
I'm an eco-freak
I'm Super Teen..."

He spat the words out, missing the beat every time. I checked out people's reactions to the rap.

I looked over at Amundson. If _he_ liked it, Ty was doomed.

Uh-oh.

"Global warming u gotta prevent it
Let's all write postcards to the —"

"That's fine!" I cut him off before he
could say the word <u>Senate</u>. Behind me, I heard
giggles and snorts of disbelief.
Ty looked startled. "Shouldn't I do the
second verse —?"
"Save it for tonight. We're short on time." I
hid behind my clipboard. The other performers
elbowed each other and whispered. Ty left the
stage quietly and sat down.
People were still talking. "Ha ha ha . . .
OMG . . . did you see his . . ."
I sank low in my seat. Seeing Ty get laughed
at wasn't as fun as I'd hoped. It was more
uncomfortable. And this was just a preview.
What would it be like tonight, with the whole
audience watching a full performance?
Too late to think about <u>that</u>.
Eager to move on, I called Quinn Romanoff,
a burly bassoon player. Since the show was heavy
on yo-yo tricks and squirt guns, I figured he'd

add a little class. When Quinn lugged a big gray metal box onstage, I was surprised. He plopped it down and uncoiled a long extension cord.

"What's in the box?" I asked.

"Fog machine," he said.

I was confused. "For a bassoon solo?"

"Yeah." Quinn nodded. "My brother said to liven it up. Make it more like a Jay-Z concert. It's going to be epic. Fog, plus some sniper fire sound effects."

While Quinn went to get his bassoon, I felt a tap on my shoulder.

"Danny?" It was Asia!

"Hey."

"Sorry to bother you," she whispered.

"'S okay." I always liked having an excuse to talk to her. She was wearing a baseball jacket, rolled up jeans, and work boots.

"I'm so glad you're doing this fund-raiser," Asia said. "The playground renovation is a great idea. During the show, I want to give a pitch for doing more projects."

"Sure. Okay." I kept my voice level, but inside I was doing a fist pump. Yes!

"There's a problem, though. . . ."

I looked at her. I suddenly realized she was really nervous about something.

"I've never given a speech before," she said. "All those people out there —" She did an exaggerated shiver. "I don't think I can do it!"

I could sense Ty listening from a few seats over. Please don't interrupt right now, I begged him silently. This was a unique moment — Asia asking my advice. It will never, ever happen again.

"Yes, you can," I said in a low voice. It felt weird — me telling someone to relax onstage. "Think of it as something you're doing for other people. It's not about you. It's for a bigger cause."

Wow — where did that come from? Asia

smiled, and my stomach dropped like I was on the Scrambler at Wild Wayne's Amusement Park.

    I looked over at Ty, who seemed lost in thought about something.

    "Hey, Danny." Quinn came up to me, breaking the spell. Holding his extension cord, he pointed to an electric socket on the side of the lighting board. "Okay if I plug in my fog machine here?"

Jasper wasn't around, and I didn't know the answer. The socket already had about five cables plugged into it. Should I try and find Jasper? Crud! I didn't want to look un-confident in front of Asia. Putting on my Talent Show Director's voice, I turned to Quinn.

"Sure," I said. "Plug it in."

About 10 seconds later, fog rolled through the auditorium, along with Bach's Étude #4, and then — THWOK! HISSSSS! POPPITY POP! POW!

Sparks shot up from the lighting board. Asia and I jumped back. "Fire!" someone shouted. The board crackled and popped. Did the fog machine overload the circuit?

Amundson ran around the room frantically.

Then all the lights went out.

* CHAPTER FIFTEEN *

A burly, red-haired fireman was on his walkie-talkie in the school lobby. "Yeah, we got a 731 at Gerald Ford Middle School, corner of Main and Dodge. 10-4."

A shorter, chubby fireman with a droopy mustache came out of the auditorium. "Who's in charge here?"

Amundson extended his arm for a handshake. "Maurice Amundson, Assistant Principal."

"We're putting on a talent show," I explained. "The lighting board must have overloaded." Guiltily, I remembered telling Quinn he could plug in his fog machine. I looked around for Asia, but didn't see her.

"We'll take a look," said the red-haired fireman. "Right now, everyone stays out here."

The performers were crowded into the lobby. We looked like some kind of crazy circus, carrying batons, tubas, rubber chickens, and a cage with a live snake.

I waved my hands. "Hey, everyone," I said. "Right now they're working on the lights, so we can't finish rehearsal. But don't worry! Everything'll go great tonight!"

Chantal and her crew were just coming down the stairs from the science lab. "Did you just say there's no rehearsal?" she asked. "I must have heard wrong."

"Little problem with the lights," I said.

"Danny." Chantal's eyes were blazing. "What kind of amateur operation are you running? That dressing room is NASTY. Da'Nise almost got her hair caught in the hamster wheel —"

Her crew joined in. "Uh-huh." "Yea-ah."

The rest of the crowd gathered around excitedly. A showdown with Chantal was <u>way</u> more entertaining than a talent show.

"Then some nerds barge in and say they want to talk about <u>spiders</u>," Chantal continued.

The Insect Club! I forgot they held meetings in the science lab. Were two more unlikely groups ever thrown together?

"Chantal." My voice was low. "Let's calm down and talk about it. By ourselves."

"I don't care who hears!" Chantal looked around. "You promised me food, drink, and a decent place to change. What'd I get? A dressing room with frogs! Nerds barging in on me!"

"We're not nerds," a guy in a reindeer sweater spoke up.

"Chantal —" I tried again.

"And now there's no rehearsal?" Chantal's voice rose even higher. "My dancers need to practice onstage. We've got complicated spotlight effects, and a light show." She shook her head in disgust. "How are we going to do that if we don't rehearse?"

"You and I —"

"I can't work under these conditions." Chantal sniffed. "I QUIT!"

Holy crud.

She whipped her cape around, put her nose in the air, and walked away, followed by her entourage.

"Oooooooooooooooh," the crowd murmured.

Jasper and I looked at each other, stunned. Then we ran after her down the hall.

"Chantal! No! Don't leave!" I shouted.

"Can't we talk about it?" begged Jasper.

Ignoring us, she crashed through the main double doors, flanked by an army of angry followers. Chantal loved dramatic exits.

"This is a disaster." I stood with Jasper at the double doors, watching Chantal disappear across the lawn. "This is huge."

"Seriously." Jasper nodded.

Even though Chantal was a pain to deal with, we needed her in the show — desperately. Why hadn't we remembered to get her those stupid snacks? Why hadn't we gotten her a dressing room...?

Ty came up behind us. "Sorry about Chantal," he said. "I mean, especially because her picture is on the poster, and all."

Thanks for reminding us.

"Yeah," I said. "It's lousy."

"But you're still going to do the show." Ty's eyes widened. "Aren't you?"

"I don't know." I looked at Jasper. "Should we?"

"Without Chantal, it's not much of a show," said Jasper. "When people find out she's not performing, they will stay home," said Jasper. "And maybe half the cast."

"That's terrible." Ty shook his head. "I wish there was something we could do." He slipped away to the hall, pulling out his phone.

Kirby Hammer came up to us. "What's happening with the show? I'm ready to blow some bubbles."

"How about my monologue?" Morgan pouted.

Jasper and I waited for the firemen to come out.

Finally the double doors opened. The red-haired guy was holding a toolbox, and the droopy mustache guy was wiping his forehead with a bandanna. They called Jasper and me over.

"This lighting board's fried," reported Droopy Mustache. "No way it'll work tonight, until someone rewires it. On Monday, the school office can call an electrician."

On Monday? But . . .

"Could you fix it?" I asked Droopy Mustache.

"No." The red-haired guy jumped in. "We can't get tied up doing favors during work hours. They need us back at the firehouse."

"So that's it? The show's off?" I asked. "There's nothing you can do?"

"Sorry, kid," he said.

Jasper and I looked at each other. That was that. I felt a wave of sadness, thinking about the moment at rehearsal when I'd felt proud of it all, seeing the show we'd put together. Now it would probably never happen.

With his phone in his hand, Ty ran up to us.

"I solved your problem." He held up his other hand. "High-five me."

We turned to stare at Ty. The firemen raised their eyebrows.

"Forget Chantal." Ty was out of breath. "You've got a new headliner: Skye Blue."

"WHAT????" Jasper and I just stood there, openmouthed.

"Skye Blue says he'll drop by the show tonight," he said. "He'll do a few tricks, make a special appearance, whatever you need."

Was he serious?

"Ty. Wow." My brain could barely absorb the news. Ty had the biggest stunt rider in the country starring in his show — and he was willing to lend him to us? "That's amazing. But we just found out —" I looked over at the firemen. "The show's cancelled."

"Light board's busted," Jasper reported sadly.

Droopy Mustache whispered something to the red-haired fireman. The red-haired fireman whispered back.

"Did you just say . . . Skye Blue? The stunt bike guy on YouTube?" Droopy Mustache cocked his head.

We nodded.

"My kid loves him," said Droopy Mustache.

"He rips it up," agreed the red-haired fireman.

"So let me get this straight," Droopy Mustache continued. "If someone did fix that board, Skye Blue would be here tonight?"

"Yup." My heart leaped.

The two firemen looked at each other.

"Hand me that wrench," said Droopy Mustache.

The firemen went back inside the auditorium, while Ty, Jasper, and I waited on a bench in the lobby. Jasper pulled out a Yoo-Hoo can, and we toasted the fireman's son, for being a fan of Skye.

"So, Ty." Jasper turned to him. "How did you get Skye to agree to drop by the talent show?"

"I told him it was a major fundraiser." Ty shrugged. "To renovate an inner city playground. I said the show was falling apart. He wanted to help."

I rubbed my knuckles, trying to take in what

Ty had done. Is he for real? I wondered. Nobody was _that_ nice.

"Ty, that's a great offer," I said slowly. "Mind-bogglingly great. But Green-a-palooza's in two weeks. If kids see Skye Blue tonight, won't that make _your_ show less of a draw?"

"I don't know." Ty bit his lip. "Maybe. But — so what? They're both good causes."

"You would really do that for us?" I didn't know if I'd do that for _anyone_. Ty's unselfishness was unsettling. It was like he was from another planet.

Ty looked at the ground. "It's funny," he said. "I actually kind of got the idea from . . . you."

"From _me_?" This was getting weirder and weirder.

"Yeah. I heard you talking to Asia," he said. "Telling her she should relax about her speech. That it wasn't about her; it was for something bigger."

Jasper rolled his eyes.

"When Chantal quit," Ty continued, "I thought I could help out."

I looked at him. My stomach suddenly felt hollow, and my mouth went dry. A strange, terrible thought ran through me like a shiver:

Maybe I'd misjudged this guy.

Sure, Ty could be a pill sometimes. But now he had done the nicest thing anyone had ever done for me, and I was going to pay him back... how?

By setting him up to be a laughingstock.

Crud.

Crud.

Triple crud.

"Hey, Mr. Producer!"

The main doors opened again and the

firemen came out. Droopy Mustache was holding a wrench.

"Just want you to know." He was out of breath. "We're still working on the lights. But I can say this. . . ."

His smile made my chest sink.

"The show is <u>definitely on</u>!"

I sighed.

"That's great news," I said glumly.

* CHAPTER SIXTEEN *

Jasper and I were backstage, sitting on a trunk marked PROPS. It was six o'clock and we could hear the firemen in the auditorium, working on the lighting board.

"You know we can't let Ty go on tonight," I said.

Jasper sighed. "I know."

For a moment, we were both quiet.

"I couldn't believe it when he offered to give us Skye," said Jasper. "I wasn't expecting that."

So Jasper felt ashamed too.

"You saw the reaction to his rap in rehearsal," I said. "And that was only singing a couple lines."

"Yeah." Jasper shifted.

"Everybody kept saying 'what's <u>wrong</u> with that guy?'"

"He's saving our butts," I said. "We've got to save his."

"Well." Jasper scratched his head. "We could tell him the truth."

The truth?

"I don't know." I shook my head.

Jasper shrugged. "Something like, 'Honestly, Ty — I don't think rapping is your thing.'"

"Jasper, it's not that simple," I said. "If we tell him his rapping is lousy now, he'll know we lied to him before."

I imagined myself in Ty's shoes. What if I'd showed someone my secret pastime, and he urged me to share it with the world? How would I feel later, finding out he'd plotted against me?

"He'd be really, really hurt," I continued. Thinking about it, I wanted to crawl into a hole and die.

"Okay. Well," said Jasper. "Got any other ideas?"

"Yeah," I said. "Cancel the show."

"WHAT?" Jasper's neck snapped up. "After

everything we
went through
today, you want
to tell people
the show's off?
What reason
would we give?"

"I dunno," I
said miserably. "We could invent something."

Haz mat emergency

Swine flu outbreak

Tsunami warning

Jasper was quiet
again. "I think you
should be honest with
Ty," he said, shaking his
head. "If you want to
try to get the show
cancelled, I'm not going
to stop you. But I'm not going to help, either."

I didn't know how to cancel the show. But I knew how to make someone else cancel it.

The light in Principal Kulbarsh's office was on.

He was a man of strong convictions. As I walked toward his door, I tried to think about things that made his nostrils twitch in anger.

* TOP FIVE BELIEFS OF PRINCIPAL KULBARSH

1. Pants shouldn't be worn below the butt.
2. No pierced belly buttons
3. "Chillax" isn't a real word
4. Students with 107 degree temperatures are faking, or dead.
5. It's not a vacation if you don't have homework.

He also believed in Setting an Example. When 12 dollars went missing from the Spring Carnival cash box, he wouldn't let the event start until the money was found. Everyone was relieved when Kiki DeFranco admitted she swiped it, and the relay races could begin.

When I got closer to the door, I heard a strange, high-pitched trilling. "Odel-Ay, Odel-Ay, Odel-Ay-EEEE-Oooo."

I waited for a break in the noise and then knocked.

"Come in," Kulbarsh called out. When I walked in, I wasn't prepared for the outfit he was wearing.

"Dr. Kulbarsh," I began. "There's . . . a thief on the loose!"

"Excuse me?" he asked.

"Seventeen dollars is missing," I said. "From the Discretionary Expense Fund!"

The "thief" was me. I had taken 17 dollars to buy Chantal snacks, and had already gotten permission for it. But technically, the money was "missing" until I produced a receipt.

"I see." The principal frowned.

"We should stop the show," I said. "Until the thief comes forward. You know, like at Spring Carnival."

Kulbarsh stood up and walked around his desk. "That is a terrible, terrible crime," he said slowly. "And punishment will be duly meted out . . ."

Yes!

He locked eyes with mine.

"...right after my performance tonight."

Wait a minute. What?

Kulbarsh opened the door for me.

"It's my day off, and I came to school to yodel," said the principal, lifting his chin. "And yodel is what I intend to do. We'll deal with the thief on Monday."

His inconsistency was infuriating. I walked away, hearing his falsetto drift down the hall.

"Odel-Ay, Odel-Ay, Odel-Ay-EEEE-Oooo!"

Q. What's the only thing harder than putting on a talent show?

A. Cancelling one.

As I left Kulbarsh's office, I tried to think of more ideas. In the lobby, I stopped the school security guard, Mr. Robinson.

"What if I told you..."

I paused and leaned on his desk. "That there might be a snake running around school?"

Mr. Robinson put down his newspaper. "Snake?"

"Becca Loomis brought it in for the show," I said. As far as I knew, it was safe backstage, but I could undo the latch on its carrier.

"You mean Pretzel?" Mr. Robinson laughed. "Chill, son. Milk snakes are harmless."

Another dead end.

I shot back to the auditorium, even more frantic. The firemen were gone. Inspecting the newly fixed lighting board, I had an evil idea:

Maybe I could overload it again.

I dashed off to the janitor's closet and hauled back as many of Ralph's appliances as I could find there, including his electric razor. If I plugged them in, maybe I'd blow the circuits.

Just as I was about to stuff the last plug into the board...

"What are you doing?"

I turned around and saw Droopy Mustache and the red-haired fireman.

"I, was, uh —" I stammered. Crud.

"Giving the thing a test run?" asked Droopy Mustache.

I looked up to see if he was angry. But his eyes were friendly.

Phew.

"Yeah." I smiled weakly.

"Don't worry." He chuckled, picking up his axe. "We rewired the board so it's twice as powerful as before." The red-haired fireman went to the corner and picked up his tool box.

Unplugging the machines, I desperately scanned the room. "Look at that garbage can blocking the exit door!" I yelled. "Isn't that a fire violation?"

The red-haired guy moved the garbage can off to the side. "Not anymore, it isn't."

I looked around for something . . . anything . . .

"How about that bundle of dusty old newspapers in the corner?" I pointed my finger.

Droopy looked over and shrugged. "Yeah? So?"

Crud! What now?

The firemen opened the door and waved good-bye. "See you shortly, kid. Good luck."

Watching them leave the auditorium, I felt frantic. My last hope for avoiding disaster was walking out with them! There was no way to reverse our terrible idea. In an hour, Ty was going to get laughed off the stage — after doing us the world's biggest favor. <u>And we can't stop it.</u>

Opening the door, I flew after the firemen.

"There might be four hundred *people* here tonight!" I yelled down the hall. "Doesn't that exceed MAXIMUM OCCUPANCY????"

But the main door clicked shut. They had already left.

* CHAPTER SEVENTEEN *

Showtime was in — gulp — 10 minutes.

The line to get into the talent show stretched into the lobby, out the door, and onto the sidewalk in front of school. Once word got around that Skye was coming, everyone stormed the place. Our security team — Axl, Boris, and Spike — had their hands full.

"Single file!" Boris shouted.

"Anyone who cuts the line..." Axl flashed an evil smile. "Gets a swirly."

"Eeeeeeeeeeew!" everyone squealed.

"Axl." I pulled him aside. "Take it down a notch. No threats. How's it going?"

"I'm keeping them in line, but..." Axl looked

around, frowning. "It'd be a lot easier if we had Tasers."

As I headed for the stage door, I overheard chatter about the show.

"... gotta see this guy ... he's unbelievable ..."

I slowed down to hear more.

"... the worst rapper ..."

"... sticking his thumbs out ..."

"... almost died laughing ..."

They were talking about Ty! Based on just a few moments at rehearsal, the whole crowd was buzzing. This was bad — <u>really</u> bad. A guy in a baseball cap held up a phone.

"I'm definitely recording him for YouTube," he said.

"Me too," said his friend.

Oh, no. No, no, no, no, <u>no</u>.

My stomach turned over. Ty on YouTube? This was turning into a disaster. When we'd urged Ty to be in the talent show, we had never meant for it to go this far.

I'd wanted to take the guy down a peg, not destroy him.

Now he was going to be the butt of some huge joke that could spread throughout the school, maybe the world.

And on the Internet, it could go on forever. Thinking about it, I felt deeply, deeply nauseous. I had to stop Ty from performing — no matter what it took.

Even telling the truth.

As I bolted through the double doors, I ran into Amundson.

"Dawg, look at all these people," he said. "You must be mad excited!"

"Yeah," I said unhappily. "It's really happening."

"Hello, ladies and germs. It is FANTASTIC to be here." Ralph, the janitor-turned-emcee, gripped the podium. He wore a glittery tuxedo with red high-tops. "Welcome to . . . the First Annual School Talent Show!"

"Woo-hoo!" "Yay!" "Woot-woot!"

Big cheers. The auditorium was so packed, it seemed like people were hanging from the ceiling. The crowd was excited. People started chanting, "Skye Blue! Skye Blue! Skye Blue!"

"We've got a GREAT show for you tonight," said Ralph. "Clog dancers. Jump ropers. Yodelers. Skateboarders. Even a rapper . . ."

The crowd shrieked with laughter, and Ralph looked surprised.

"Okay," he said. "Glad you're looking forward to that. We just added a surprise act at the end, and — a VERY SPECIAL GUEST . . ."

The crowd went nuts.

"SKYE! SKYE! SKYE! SKYE!"

"So without further ado, I'd like to introduce our first performers . . . Peter and the Laff Riots!"

From backstage, I watched the guys run out with their squirt guns. Ty was scheduled to go on third. That meant I had just a few minutes to find him and bodily prevent him from going onstage.

"Has anyone seen Ty?"

I ran past banjo players, yo-yo-ists, hula-hoopists. Nobody knew where he was.

I poked my head into the boys' bathroom. The more places I looked, the more frantic I got.

He wasn't in the wings, or hallway, or the lobby. I opened the door to check the "Green Room" again, the space adjoining the stage, where the performers warmed up. Inside, I hit a huge wall of people gathered around someone. They were shouting questions:

"Are you going to do a backflip off the wall?"

"Was that your dog in the video?"

"How many bikes do you have?"

I jumped up to see over the crowd and spotted a guy with wild blond hair tucked under a beanie.

Skye Blue was in da' house.

Normally, I'd be over there drooling with the rest of the pack, but I had to find Ty. I skirted around the edge of the mob, but Milo, our stage manager,

grabbed me. "Danny! You've got to meet someone!"

He pulled me in, and the crowd parted. Suddenly I was standing in front of Skye Blue, everyone's hero.

My hero.

Skye had piercing blue eyes and tanned skin. A Chinese character was tattooed on his wrist. He had a dangerous anything-could-happen gleam in his eyes.

"So you're the dude who put this whole show together." He smiled at me.

"Um. Yeah." My eyes scanned the room for Ty.

"Cool." Skye nodded. "I thought I'd do a Leap of Death, with a switchback down the ramp. Then a Flamingo or a Candy Bar, maybe even a —"

"Whatever. Sounds great," I said, cutting him off. I turned and ran, leaving shocked faces all around me. I couldn't believe I was ditching Skye Blue! But I didn't have time for him now —

I had to find Ty.

As I flew down the hall behind the stage, Chantal grabbed me. In her gold-sequined top, she was clearly dressed to perform. Now that Skye was on board, I knew she wanted back in. She grabbed my arm.

"Not now, Chantal," I said.

"Skye Blue's here, right?" Her eyes lit up. "Doing the show?"

"I don't have time to talk —"

"Danny." Her voice was pleading. "Don't mess with me."

"You said you'd never be in one of my shows again," I said.

"Hrrmph." Chantal squirmed.

"Look, Chantal, I've got to find Ty —"

"Dang it, Danny." Chantal threw down her giant purse. "What do I have to do? Get down on my knees and lick your sorry no-name sneakers?"

I pretended to consider it.

"Naw, that's okay, Chantal," I said. "We'll put you back in."

"Yay!" she shouted. "Ladies, haul your shaggy butts in here. We've got a show to do!"

Five minutes to find Ty.

Running around, I spotted Jasper on a ladder.

"Jasper!" I panted. "Where's Ty?"

He climbed down. "I dunno. Why?"

"Word got out about his rap," I whispered. "People can't wait to see him bomb! Between him and Skye Blue? He's the bigger attraction."

Jasper shook his head. "Oh, no. Geez."

"It gets worse," I continued. "People are planning to record his rap and put it on YouTube."

Jasper groaned. "He's on in..." He checked his watch. "Three minutes."

Crud! I did one more frantic spin backstage and then —

Out of the corner of my eye, I spotted someone heading for the wings. "TY!" I yell-whispered.

"Danny!" Ty walked toward me, and I practically tackled him.

"Where were you?" I was relieved. "I looked all over —"

"I was in the science lab," he said. "Thinking. I don't know about doing this rap, Danny. People had a weird reaction to it."

"Uh-huh." I looked at the floor.

"I'm probably just nervous, right?" He chuckled. "It's important to get my message out there. And you think it's good. If it weren't for you, I wouldn't be doing this."

Milo walked by. "You're on in one minute, Ty."

Say it. Now.

"Don't do it." I blurted out.

"WHAT?" He blinked.

"I led you wrong." I swallowed.

"But..." Ty's face darkened. "In the locker room, you said —"

"I lied," I said flatly.

"You wanted me in the show....." Ty's voice was fierce. "You begged me."

"Because it was a terrible rap," I said miserably. "I was mad at you. We wanted to show everyone."

Ty looked at me stunned, now taking in the full horror of it. It was the worst moment of my life.

"Who else is in on the joke?" He said quietly. "The whole school?"

When I didn't say anything, he squeezed his eyes shut. Beat me up, I begged silently. I deserve it! I'd rather have Axl punch my lights out a million times than look at Ty's unhappy face a moment longer.

He didn't lunge at me, though. Instead his shoulders went slack, and he just kind of crumpled.

Which was a thousand times worse. I felt like the lowest form of life imaginable.

"Ty." Milo came up and pointed. "You're on."

* CHAPTER EIGHTEEN *

Someone had to make the announcement.

I walked out onstage and stepped up to the microphone. The glare of the lights was overwhelming. Shielding my eyes with my hand, I squinted at hundreds of people.

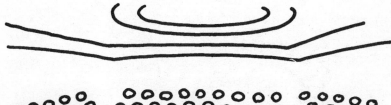

Looking at me. Waiting.

Ty Randall won't be performing tonight. I opened my mouth to say the words, but nothing came out. Looking over in the wings, I saw Ty slumped in his chair. What had I done? Could I ever make it right?

My hands were sweating. At the foot of the stage, one of the stage crew guys held up a cue card with Ty's lyrics on it.

The music track came on, startling me. BOOM-DIDDA-BOOM. BOOM-DIDDA-BOOM. BOOM-DIDDA-BOOM...

I started to say, "Turn off the music!" But glancing into the wings again, I saw Ty sitting with his head in his hands, trying to accept the idea that someone <u>wanted</u> him to make a fool of himself.

I took a deep breath, and looked at the cue card. With shaking arms, I lifted the mike to my lips.

"'Cuz I'm mean
I'm green
I'm an eco-freak
I'm Super Teen..."

My voice cracked. If you're going to do it, I told myself, do it all the way. I started swinging my arms overhead, like the rappers on TV.

"Global warming u gotta
prevent it
    Let's all write postcards
to the Senate. . . ."

    People started to laugh.
Although my brain must have
known this could happen,
hearing their ha ha has hit
me like a punch in the
stomach. I look every bit as
ridiculous as Ty, I thought. I could see people
laughing so hard they were doubled over.

A few hours ago, I would have said this was my worst nightmare. But the moment I'd told Ty the truth was far, far worse.

> "If the ice cap melts, it's gonna get tragic
> Ocean levels rise like magic . . ."

The real me was floating overhead somewhere, looking down on myself flailing around. The audience glittered with dozens of shiny objects — cell phones held up to catch the moment for eternity.
"Booooo! Booooo!"
The crowd was getting rowdier. Why had I started singing? Was I out of my mind? This was a total freakin' nightmare, but now that I had started, I didn't know how to stop.
"You reek! Go home!"

Now people were stomping their feet. PLONK! Someone lobbed a water bottle on stage. BLATT! Someone else threw a sandwich.

"Ha ha ha ha ha..." Laughter swelled again after someone pelted me with an open bag of Skittles.

Could a person actually die of embarrassment? My breath started to come in ragged bursts, and I didn't know if I could keep going. My voice got thick, and my knees started to buckle....

"'Cause I'm...mean...I'm...green..."

"DU-U-U-U-U-U-U-U-DE...!!!"

Who was that? Suddenly, something shot out of the wings. Was it a bird? Was it a plane? No, it was...

Skye Blue, riding his bike full speed.

The cyclist flew onto the stage, and circled around me. Then Skye leaned back into a wheelie, hopping up and down on the rear wheel. I watched in amazement as he bounced across the floor, using the rear wheel like a pogo stick.

The audience gasped. He circled around me again and did a backflip off the wall.

"SKYE!" More cheers, screams, foot stomps. Skye rolled back across the stage, and then ditched the bike and joined me. He put his hand on my shoulder and bent toward the mike.

"Hey, people!" Skye took the mike. "This rap is SICK! He's got a slammin' message, and I'm behind him ALL THE WAY." He gave his devilish, crooked smile. "We all are! If you want more bike tricks, stand up and REPEAT AFTER ME!"

Skye called out lines from the cue card. "I'm mean, I'm green —"

People sang tentatively.

"Louder, people!" Skye roared. "I can't HEAR you!"

"I'M MEAN, I'M GREEN, I'M AN ECO-FREAK, I'M SUPER TEEN ..." the audience yelled.

"I. CAN'T. HEAR. YOU!" Skye hollered.

This time, they screamed. Skye started clapping above his head, and the audience joined in. After his stunts, he could have flogged himself with a dead fish, and people would have copied him.

I looked over in the wings for Ty. He was standing up now, nodding his head, and almost . . . smiling.

Relief surged through me. I motioned for him to join us, but he looked hesitant. Other performers were flooding onstage, jumping at the chance to join Skye.

Not to be outdone, Chantal pushed her way through and planted herself next to me and Skye.

"Mackin' on a fuel . . . that's renewable
C'mon, people . . . it's way <u>do-able</u>"

In a thousand years, I'd never have imagined Chantal leading the crowd in a song about biofuels. But her showstopping voice and sassiness took the rap to a whole new level. We

all moved back to make room for her, and she
started adding her own words.

   "Wake up, people, will you? We got to do
something about this problem, and I mean now.
You think we got twenty years to figure this
out? I got news for you, girlfriend." She put her
hands on her hips. "WE DON'T. And if the
politicians can't get off their bony butts, let's
take the matter into our own hands. Let me
hear you say yeah."
   "YEAH!" the crowd shouted back.
   "Yeah!" Chantal roared.
   "YEAH!" The crowd shouted harder.
   "YeeeeaaaaaaaaaaAHHHHHHHHHHHHHHH!"
Chantal extended the word, holding the note

until she was red in the face. The event had transformed into a gospel show/rap contest/ protest rally.

Talk about getting your message out!

Who would have pegged Chantal as an environmental crusader? But her bullying style worked perfectly. When the song finished, we all took a bow. Glancing at Ty in the wings, I saw him clapping for us. I felt like I would burst with relief and amazement.

Leaving the stage, I could hear music from the next act, a modern dance piece called "Inspirations." When I got to the wings, Jasper ran up and pulled me over. "Danny." He was out of breath. "<u>Holy crud.</u> Are you out of your mind?" he asked.

I looked at the ground. "Maybe a little."

"You sure got lucky." Jasper whistled.

I nodded.

"Skye saved my butt." I shuddered, remembering all those phones in the air, recording it. "And could you believe Chantal?"

"Who's talking about me?" Chantal came up to us, patting her forehead with a cotton ball. A slim boy followed her, carrying a bottle of something pink and strong-smelling.

"You were awesome." I bowed down to the queen. "You should work for the Environmental Protection Agency."

"Tell them to call my agent. I

have to get ready for _my_ number," she said airily. She walked off in a flock of girls in glittery outfits.

"Hey, Danny." Axl pushed his way backstage. "I didn't know you rapped. I thought that other dork was supposed to —"

"I did it for him."

"Yeah, okay." Axl chuckled. "It doesn't matter which dweeb gets up there. Neither of you is Killa Whale." He loved to mention his favorite rapper. I pictured myself on his CD.

"The show's not as bad as I thought it would be," Axl admitted, nodding a little. "But if you had let in <u>our</u> band?" He gave an insane cackle. "Mutilator would have brought down the house."

Literally, I thought.

I went over to the wings, and peeked out onstage. A skateboarder was flying down a ramp, while a graffiti art slideshow flickered on the wall behind him. Now that Skye and Chantal had energized the audience, they were hooting and clapping for everyone.

I felt a tug on my shirt.

"I did it!" said Asia. "Did you hear my speech?"

"Oh, no! I forgot!" It must have been while I was talking to Jasper and Axl backstage!

"It went fine. Seeing you up there made me less nervous," she said.

"Yeah?" I was afraid to hear more. I didn't want to think about her being in the audience.

"You're not a very good rapper," Asia said matter-of-factly. "But you didn't let that stop you."

Ouch.

"Instead, you got a whole roomful of people singing about global warming. So cool! Besides..." she leaned in. "I heard what everyone said about Ty at rehearsal. You did him a big favor going on in his place."

Now I felt uncomfortable. It was one thing to get props for being willing to look stupid just to keep the show going. It was another to accept credit for being such a good friend to Ty.

"You know, Asia," I said in a low voice. "I wasn't so great to Ty. I got him to rap in the show because it was the one thing he wasn't good at. I wanted everyone to see that."

Asia's mouth was open. But I had to keep going.

"When we got to rehearsal, I knew I'd messed up. I felt so bad, I ended up doing the

rap myself. So . . ." I looked at the floor. "Now you know."

Asia fell silent. "I'm surprised, Danny."

More waves of shame. I didn't tell her what had really turned me against Ty in the first place: that he seemed like the kind of guy that she would like. Once that thought took hold, pretty much anything Ty did was wrong.

ASIA'S DREAM GUY

"I'm really sorry." The words hung there for a moment. As they echoed in my brain, I realized I had to say them to someone else.

"Excuse me, Asia." I pointed across the room. "I've got to —"

"Bye, Danny." She hesitated, then added, "Thanks for telling me what happened. At least you tried to make it right in the end."

"Yeah," I said. "But I still have more to do."

Up onstage, T-Bone Farrell was spinning on his head.

I slipped off to the "Green Room," where I found Ty in a group gathered around Skye. When Skye saw me, he slapped me on the back. "Great rap, kid."

"Tell <u>him</u> that," I pointed to Ty. "He wrote it."

"You did?" Skye turned and offered his hand for a fist-bump. "It's awesome."

"Thanks." Ty bumped him back, half-smiling.

Skye looked at the other kids. "I hope you guys really listened to the lyrics. Global warming is no joke." Then Skye turned to me. "And you . . . um, you were brave to get out there."

"Hey, Danny," Pinky Shroeder called out with a snicker. "Don't quit your day job!"

My face felt hot. I was getting tired of the "ha-ha-weren't-you-terrible" remarks.

"Dude, no one expects you to be a great rapper," Skye said, and then he turned to Ty. "Or you, either. How could you be? Getting good at something takes practice. You think I was born knowing how to do a one-handed Superman wheelie? I practice stunts every day, for hours."

"Danny's been busy drawing." Emma pointed to the Green-a-palooza poster on the wall.

"You did this?" Skye turned to look at the poster. "It rocks!"

In spite of everything, I was pleased that Skye liked my work.

"Hey, Skye!"

"SKYE!"

The cyclist went off to greet more fans. Ty and I were left staring at each other awkwardly. This was my moment to say something, but I didn't know where to start.

"Hey, Ty," I began.

"Hey," he mumbled.

"I'm sorry about . . . you know." I looked at

the floor. "I don't know why it happened. You were just so, you know, perfect all the time."

What was I — a girl?

"Perfect?!" He laughed bitterly. "Hah!"

"Well, you are," I said.

"Hardly." He lifted his chin. "You're an artist. You drew 'I Was a Preteen Cyclops.' You directed the talent show. And you know tons of people."

Sort of true, I realized. Chantal, Axl, Asia, the lunch table girls, tech nerds. It was a strange mix, but they added up.

"You save wounded animals," I accused him. "You play soccer and Frisbee, and put on Green-a-palooza, and had a skateboard recycling drive —"

"How'd you know that?" He looked puzzled.

Oops. The skateboard recycling was at his old school — Jasper learned that when he tried to dig up dirt on him. "Um — never mind," I said. "The point is — you built a solar oven to bake pizza and you . . ."

We looked at each other and laughed.

"Listen to us." I shook my head, embarrassed.

"I never meant to broadcast that stuff," Ty said. "Being new and all, maybe I . . . tried too hard."

We both looked at the floor.

Why had Ty bugged me so much? Somehow he'd become the focus of all our frustrations. All I could see were Ty's successes, everywhere. My jealousy had really messed me up. Even if Ty hadn't turned out to be a nice guy, why had I done something like that to anyone?

"I'm sorry about everything," I continued. "I'd take it back if I could. Maybe we could just . . . start over?"

Ty nodded. "Yeah."

We were both quiet.

"C'mon," I said. "Let's go watch the rest of the show."

* * *

"Odel-Ay, Odel-Ay, Odel-Ay-EEEE-Oooo."

Dr. Kulbarsh was yodeling his head off. Just the sight of him in lederhosen and a cap was astonishing enough. Everyone stared, amazed.

"And the lonely goatherd sang 'Odel-ay, odel-ay, odel-ay, odel-ay eeee-Oooo!'"

Ralph the emcee held up his hands and clapped. "when Dr. Kulbarsh took the stage," he confided to the audience, "I thought, 'Not another yodeling principal!' But this guy's good!"

Ty and I laughed. The energy level of the show kept rising, as we watched the rowdy audience cheer and scream for every act — from the snake whisperer, to the soccer ball bouncer, to the water-glass rock star. When Chantal came on, she took the show up three more notches.

"Gerald Ford Middle School!" she yelled. "Make some NOISE!"

Her dancers lifted her up so she floated like a balloon in the Macy's parade. Just when the excitement couldn't get any higher...

Skye Blue burst onstage.

He did a wheelie, then he rotated the bike 360 degrees. Our jaws dropped as he dazzled us with one trick after another after another.

Jasper came up behind me and Ty, and we all gawked together.

Skye Blue ended in a spin. With the audience still gasping, he got off his bike and took the mike.

"This school ROCKS!" Skye yelled. "This playground project is so cool, I'm going to kick in 2,500 dollars. Plus, I want all the kids at Gerald Ford AND P.S. 160 to be my guests for a day at Big Kahuna Water Park!"

"YAY!!!!" The audience roared.

Jasper and I looked at each other, astonished. Big Kahuna Water Park! That was our dream. How did Skye know...?

"I told him your original idea," said Ty.

"The Twisted Tunnel of Terror!" Jasper high-fived me.

"Honolulu Hurricane!" I fived back.

We rushed onstage with the rest of the cast, crew, and maybe half the audience to sing the rap again. Ty came too.

And you know what? He wasn't all that bad. This time, maybe he was less nervous. Not that anyone noticed — we were too busy screaming at the top of our lungs:

"I'm mean, I'm green..."

No words ever sounded better to me.

<u>H.N. KOWITT</u> has written more than forty books for younger readers, including <u>The Loser List</u>, <u>Dracula's Decomposition Book</u>, <u>This Book is a Joke</u>, and <u>The Sweetheart Deal</u>. She lives in New York City, where she enjoys cycling, flea markets, and gardening on her fire escape. You can find her online at <u>www.kowittbooks.com</u>.